Boothill Bound

When Jack Drago arrives in Tomb Valley, he is following a dream. Tired of cattle drives and bunkhouses, he is looking forward to staking a claim to the valley's free range. But the Skeltons have different ideas, which they make known very forcefully only minutes after Drago's arrival.

Because word has it that Marshal Haskin is a fair man, Drago looks to him for help. Instead, he finds a broken reed, a man who has opted out, leaving Skelton to run the town.

Then Jack meets Beth Crofton, a Skelton by birth, and there is an instant rapport between them. But this is soon to prove even more of a problem than staking a claim to some free range. Only guns and flying lead will solve it.

Boothill Bound

RIO BLANE

A Black Horse Western

ROBERT HALE · LONDON

© James O'Brien 2002
First published in Great Britain 2002

ISBN 0 7090 7121 3

Robert Hale Limited
Clerkenwell House
Clerkenwell Green
London EC1R 0HT

The right of James O'Brien to be identified as
author of this work has been asserted by him
in accordance with the Copyright, Design and
Patents Act 1988.

Typeset by
Derek Doyle & Associates, Liverpool.
Printed and bound in Great Britain by
Antony Rowe Limited, Wiltshire

For Nora K.
Missing you still.

PROLOGUE

The wind blowing off the snow-capped mountains marking the southern boundary of the valley had the sharpness of a knife-blade to it. It was a fickle wind. Gusting. Lulling. Curling. Whatever position Jack Drago settled in on his saddle, it took no time at all for the wind to find a way through the long bearskin coat he wore.

It was late Fall, with the bite of an early winter. It was the wrong time to have arrived, but his route from Abilene had been obstacle-strewn, his luck as fickle as the wind which now buffeted him.

He drew rein, his eyes wandering across and along the valley to the wooded slopes on the far hills. It was a good valley. A place where a man could put down roots, raise kids and love a wife. Its soil would be rich – its crops and grass lush. Right now the grass, what was left after winter feed had been gathered in, was a brassy yellow, not pretty in itself, but matched with the wine and gold of the Fall foliage, the overall picture rested easy on Drago's eyes. Come spring it would be shamrock green, and the twin streams that tumbled down, through ancient rocks to cut the valley would flow freely and fill the valley with the music of their ripple. Now they were beginning to show the diamond-hard brightness of frost. The earth, too, was beginning to lose its soft sponginess. Soon the valley would be covered with winter snows, already there in the low rolling clouds and likely to spill from them any time now.

'Ain't got a pretty name, I reckon,' Art Leary's voice drifted through time to Jack Drago. 'Tomb Valley. But it sure settles a man's mind to rest easy, Jack.'

Drago smiled reflectively.

'Sure does, Art,' he murmured. 'Sure does.'

'Wyomin', Jack,' Art Leary would sigh, when they'd sit around a camp-fire during a cattle drive. 'Now, that's God's own country.' He'd laugh with a toothless grin and advise, 'If you ever get the urge in you to settle down, Jack, there's this valley I come 'cross once in my restless travels, near a town called Abbot Creek. You head there. In that valley you'll find your soul again,' Art Leary had promised him. 'Some day I'm headin' back that way,' he'd say, dreamily, when reaching the end of another cattle drive. 'Mebbe this time, I'll just keep on goin' from Abilene, Jack.'

8

Boothill Bound

A week later in Abilene, at the end of the Double R drive, Art Leary fell to a fast gun. There was little or nothing in the poker pot to argue about, but the kid didn't need much of an excuse, killing being a pleasure to him that was greater than cards or women.

'You're cheating, old man!'

Jack Drago had heard the youngster's snarling accusation. He had spun round from the bar, but he was too late. The youngster had blasted Art Leary clean out of his chair and out through the window of the Lucky Ace saloon. Drago had called the youngster and killed him. But the kid's death was no consolation for the loss of the best friend he had had since the cradle. Art Leary had been all of twenty-five years older than him, a gap which should have set them apart. But it had not. And it was not a father and son relationship either. Art Leary and he had been trail friends in the best sense of the word.

The same day he had walked behind the hearse carrying Art Leary's body to Abilene's boot hill which, then, had a constant stream of mourners coming and going. In Abilene men died quick, and mostly young.

Jack Drago had been Art Leary's only mourner on that rain-sodden afternoon. He had spoken some words, as he might have if Art and he were nestling down round a camp-fire before turning in

9

for the night; words of hope and optimism. Like many men after the bloody carnage of the Civil War, Drago had forgotten how to pray in the way that Bible-school had taught him to. And if he had prayed in that way, Art Leary would probably have laughed anyway. Because he was a man who had long ago broken off communication with God, and would not now have expected God to listen to any pleading words on his part. But Drago reckoned that God had not judged Art Leary too unkindly. His life might not have been one of prayerful submission, but it had been one of caring deeds and kind words.

He was walking down the hill from the cemetery, with yet another funeral on its way up, that of the kid, when Art Leary's spirit had spoken in his ear.

'Wyomin', Jack. God's own country.'

He had decided there and then. He had driven the last cow he was going to drive for the Double R, or any other outfit. He had had enough of cows, anyway, dumb, ornery critters that they were. He would head to Wyoming and raise crops. It was what his father had done before him. It was what he would do now. And the only cow in sight would be the one which would provide the milk he'd need for drinking and making butter and cheese.

He would head for Abbot Creek.

But first he would, he decided, bust Hank

Rickard's jaw. The penny-pinching Double R boss had ordered his entire outfit out of Abilene, and had not allowed them the time to attend Art Leary's funeral.

Jack Drago had found Rickard in bed, tasting the delights of a saloon dove, and had beaten him near senseless. Then he had mounted up and ridden away from Abilene to the new life that Art Leary had said would be his, once he reached Wyoming.

Looking out across the valley which had, moments before, taken his breath away, he murmured, 'You were right, Art. This *is* God's own country.'

The sighing wind, Jack Drago reckoned, held a sigh of ghostly contentment. Drago knew that, though Art Leary's bones might be back in Abilene, his spirit was right alongside him.

ONE

Drago scooped up a handful of the creek's sweet water. He had the water to his lips when the sound of clipping hoofs interrupted his drinking. Three riders came fast out of the trees on the opposite side of the creek, two of them older than the one leading the charge, a fiery-eyed youngster whose face held the hue of a man permanently in anger. The riders clattered across the creek, and Drago had to side-step quickly to avoid being brushed aside by the leader's black stallion – a horse that seemed to match perfectly its rider's temperament.

'You're trespassing, mister,' the young man ranted. 'Git!'

'Now,' one of the older men added. 'Unless you want to be strung up!'

The third rider, the most senior of the trio, seemed to be of a calmer disposition. 'Fill your canteen and move on, stranger,' he said, not unkindly.

The leader of the group kicked the canteen which Drago had been about to replenish out of his hands. 'Water's private, too.'

Jack Drago curbed his fiery urge to drag the young man from his horse and lay into him. The man who had warned him to move on or be strung up, unerringly read Drago's urge and put a boot on his chest to pitch him backwards against a tree trunk. This action amused the youngster, but troubled the man who had spoken kindly to Drago. The young man's amusement was short-lived – anger again soured his face.

'Grab him!' he ordered his two sidekicks. 'I figure this one needs to be taught that a man doesn't enter Bent Bough range uninvited.'

The oldest of the trio said, 'A man has to know the rules before he can be punished for breaking them, Rick.'

'You draw your dollars from Sam Skelton, Ned,' Rick snarled. 'So you'll damn well do his bidding to earn them.'

'Maybe your father would want this handled differently, Rick,' Ned said, in a quiet and measured tone.

Rick Skelton sneered.

'If my pa was here, this interloper would be skinned 'live by now.'

Ned Rawlson had been with the Bent Bough right from the first steer, and had been Sam

13

Skelton's long-time confidant. They'd shared the hard times and enjoyed the good times. Sam, longer in the tooth than Rawlson by a decade, had, in recent times, spoken to his foreman about relaxing his claim to all of the valley. Recently, during a bout of supping whiskey with him, Sam had said:

'The march of time softens a man, Ned, when he realizes that important though the range is, he'll eventually have to settle for a small patch of it, no matter how many acres he owned.'

'You'll ride on when you've filled that canteen, won't you mister?'

There was a plea in Rawlson's grey eyes, that Drago would have liked to concede to. But lying was not his way.

'This is free range for any man to stake his claim to. I figure on doing just that.'

'Hear that, old man?' Rick Skelton goaded Rawlson.

Lightning quick, Rick swung his leg over his horse, inches from Jack Drago's face. He was fortunate that the silver spur which Skelton sported did not pluck his right eye from its socket. Equally as quickly, before Drago could gather his wits, Rick Skelton's backer slid from his saddle, a cocked six-gun drawn and held on Drago.

'Good work, Jake,' he complimented his cohort. Skelton's glance Ned Rawlson's way held a rattler meanness. 'Pa ain't going to like the way you stood by, Ned.'

Skelton grabbed a bull-whip that was curled around his saddle horn and unfurled it, its vicious lash cutting the air.

'Time you learned that lesson now, mister,' he said with waspish spite. 'And I aim to teach you good.'

'Whup him to a standstill, Rick,' Jake urged. 'And I'll take a piece of the action, too.'

Slowly, cherishing each second of the pleasure of what was to come, the young man settled his stance. Drago, with nothing to lose, kicked out at Skelton's knee. His right leg buckled and he toppled Drago's way. Quick as a rattler's spit, Drago looped an arm around Rick Skelton's neck in a stranglehold and used him as a shield, positioning the rancher between him and the Bent Bough hands, shifting him to counter the double threat for the couple of seconds it took him to jab a cocked pistol in Rick Skelton's spine.

'Drop your guns!' Drago ordered the men.

'Rick?' Jake whined. 'What'll I do, Rick?'

'You'll drop your damn iron, Jake,' Ned Rawlson growled. He unbuckled his own gunbelt and dropped it.

'Do as he says,' Rick Skelton instructed his backer.

15

Jake, robbed of his pleasure, was in an unpredictable and snarling mood.

'I'll drop your boss,' Drago warned.

'You do,' Skelton spat, 'and you'll never leave this valley.'

'Maybe,' Jack Drago conceded. 'But it won't matter none to you, mister.'

Drago could feel the wobble in Rick Skelton's legs.

'Drop it, Jake.' Skelton's order was now more of a plea. Jake's six-gun clattered to the ground. 'You've bought yourself a whole mess of trouble, stranger,' Skelton promised Jack Drago.

Drago backed to his horse, dragging the hapless rancher with him. He kicked back, bringing sharp pain to Drago's features as one of the silver spurs he wore scraped his shinbone. He tightened his grip on Skelton, until he gagged for breath.

'Stand right where you are,' he ordered the Bent Bough hands, and held his gun to Rick Skelton's head as he climbed aboard his horse.

Yielding to impulse, Jake foolishly dived for his discarded gun. Drago's .45 exploded. Jake was pitched back into the creek, shards of glistening bone spraying out from his shattered shoulder. The water of the creek ran red. Jake curled up in howling pain.

Taking advantage of the diversion, Rick Skelton swung about. Jack Drago's gun-butt hammered against the rancher's cheek bone. The blow spun him off balance, and he fell heavily against a boulder. Jack Drago's gun was levelled on him.

'Leave it be, stranger,' Ned Rawlson asked.

Drago uncocked his six-gun.

'Seeing that you took no part in this, I'm ready to listen.'

Nursing his badly bruised cheek, his eyes holding a hellish fire, Rick Skelton vowed: 'You're a deadman, mister.'

'I didn't come seeking trouble,' Drago chillingly replied. 'But if it comes looking for me, I'll deal with it. Of that you can be sure.'

'You know who I am?' Rick Skelton snarled.

'Don't care,' Drago said.

'My pa owns this valley,' Rick shouted after the departing Drago.

'The north end of this valley is open range,' Drago said tersely. 'And this is the north end.'

'Pa ain't going to tolerate no damn interloper. You'll find out soon enough. You're Boothill bound, mister.'

Drago drew rein. When he spoke his voice had steel in it. 'You tell your pa that what goes for you goes for him, too. My advice is, don't come looking.'

Drago led his horse up out of the creek, keeping a watchful eye, his hand in a claw ready to draw the walnut-handled Colt on his right hip.

'Like I said, mister,' Rick Skelton screamed after him. 'You're Boothill bound!'

Drago allowed the mare to find its own way up the bank of the creek into the trees, not relaxing for a second. Once in the trees, he could not relax either. A movement of undergrowth had him swinging in his saddle, his .45 sweeping from its holster.

'That was a damn fool thing to do under the circumstances,' he snarled at the woman who emerged from the undergrowth, cradling a Winchester. 'You'd be?' he enquired testily.

'Beth Crofton.'

'You saw what happened just now?'

'I saw.'

'But didn't help.'

'Didn't reckon you needed any help.'

'I might have done,' Drago said.

'Then I'd have helped, I guess.'

Drago snorted. 'You don't sound too sure about that. You live in the valley, Miss Crofton?'

'That would be Mrs Crofton.'

Jack Drago was at a loss as to why it should matter that Beth Crofton was married – but it did.

'Mrs Crofton,' he corrected.

'Yes. South end. Best range there is.'

'Better than what I've seen already?'

'That depends on how long you've been looking, Mr...?'

'Drago. Jack Drago.'

18

She held out a hand to shake. Drago shook. The woman's handshake was warm and friendly, but rough to the touch. Beth Crofton's hands were used to hard work. Her eyes, dancing pools of green, considered Drago.

'So, you're thinking of putting down roots in the valley, Mr Drago?'

'You've got good ears. And I'd be pleased if you'd call me Jack … Beth.'

She shrugged, as if it did not matter whether they remained formal or casual. But Beth Crofton sure liked the sound of her name coming from Jack Drago's lips.

'That's how I'm planning,' he confirmed.

'Good with that gun?' Beth asked.

He smiled. 'I know which end the bullets come from.'

She returned his smile.

'I suppose you've got sense enough in that black-thatched skull of yours to know that settling in what the Skeltons' reckon is their valley, every blade of grass that is, is going to bring you a whole mess of grief?'

'I've got that message, Beth.'

'Then ride on, Jack,' she said. 'Almost every place you put your foot on in the valley, you'll be standing on someone who made the same mistake you're about to make. Thinking that they could defy Sam Skelton and live to tell about it.'

19

Drago considered her advice.

'It'll save you being planted. Like all the others were, Jack.'

His name, spoken by Beth Crofton had a musical ring to it. Drago told himself that, at thirty-five years of age, he was long past being sentimental about how a woman spoke his name; such was for boys. Well, he had to admit that right now, if that were true, there was a whole lot of *boy* in him.

'I reckon my mind's made up, Beth,' he said. 'I'm staying.'

Beth Crofton had mixed feelings. She found herself wanting Jack Drago to stay, while at the same time she feared for his well-being. Emotions which, Drago being a total stranger, she should not be feeling.

Drago had dreamed of the valley on the long trek from Abilene too much to let go of that dream now. It was a dream that had taken as firm a root as a hundred-year-old oak; a dream which he would fulfil, or stop breathing in the attempt.

'Guess I'll just have to take the risk of ruffling Skelton feathers.' Drago's slate-grey eyes considered Beth Crofton. 'You don't seem to fear the Skeltons, Beth? They don't kill women?' He grinned. 'Maybe I should wear a petticoat?'

'Oh, killing a woman wouldn't give Sam or Rick Skelton any sleepless nights.'

'Then how come…?'

Beth said: 'Killing family is different.'

Drago was knocked back.

'Family?'

Beth Crofton enjoyed Drago's discomfort.

'My maiden name is Skelton, Jack. Rick is my half-brother.' Her voice was tinged with bitterness. 'The issue of my father's shacking up with a saloon whore.' Now she became sadly reflective. 'I didn't quite fit the bill. Pa wanted a boy.

'When my ma couldn't have any more children after the terrible time she had giving birth to me in the back of a wagon on the trek here, Pa sought his comforts in the Silver Mustang saloon.'

The memories reflected in Beth Crofton's green eyes made them cold and hostile, and gave her features a bitter twist.

'Ma's dead now. Died ten years ago. She wasn't really sick. She just lost the will to fight Sam Skelton any more.'

She spoke of her father as if he were a complete and utter stranger.

'A year after that I married the first man who came along. That was Ben Crofton.' She shivered, as a curl of bitter wind swept by. She looked to the leaden sky seeping down from the mountains and creeping over the valley. 'It'll snow soon, I reckon.'

'Sure has the bite of snow,' Drago agreed.

'You heading back to town?' Beth enquired.

21

'Guess so.'

'It'll be a bitter ride.'

'I've had bitter rides before, Beth.'

'You're welcome to bunk down in my barn,' she invited. 'Ride back to town tomorrow. Share what we have to offer.'

Drago was undecided. Though the prospect of spending a while longer in Beth Crofton's company greatly appealed to him, he could see his visit creating all sorts of problems. His own, he could handle. But he didn't want his troubles becoming Beth's troubles too.

'I appreciate the offer, Beth. But—'

'One more night won't make any difference, Jack,' she interjected, driven by a sudden desire to retain this interesting stranger's company for a spell longer. Unwisely so, of course. Ben Crofton was a jealous man, and there could be no doubt as to how her hospitality would be viewed by Sam and Rick Skelton. It would be viewed as an outright rejection of their quest to keep Tomb Valley their sole domain. And a total endorsement of Jack Drago's challenge, and his right to claim his share of the valley's free range.

Against his better judgement, Drago set aside his qualms.

'I guess not,' he said.

Beth Crofton felt her heart stagger. Jack Drago's lopsided grin had a mighty appealing quality. She chided herself for the silly, girlish notions filling her head; notions that should not be there in the first place, she being a married woman.

As they crossed the valley to the Crofton place, they came under the scrutiny of keen, watching eyes; eyes filled with spite. Rick Skelton was not used to being humiliated, the way Jack Drago had belittled him. He continuously stirred trouble both on the range and in town, but most men, and women too, on the receiving end of the spite, which rose with the slightest provocation, either backed off or took their beating. Because any man who bucked a Skelton in Abbot Creek was a man doomed to be run off at best, and planted at worst.

Sam Skelton had passed on his mean nature to his bastard son, and was therefore incapable of seeing any wrong-doing by him, irrespective of how unjust or brutal Rick Skelton's behaviour was. Although, recently, folk had observed a mellowing of Sam Skelton's black-hearted nature, while Rick Skelton's ire seemed to be rising in direct ratio to Sam Skelton's increasing tolerance.

On their way, Drago took Beth Crofton to the spot for which he planned to file claim. It was a sweeping expanse of range that ran to a stream to the south, and was protected by a pine-clad hill to the north.

'Should give good cover from the icy winter

winds,' he told Beth, pointing to the trees.

'That it will, if …'

'If?' Drago prompted.

'Oh, never mind,' Beth said.

'If I'm still around?' Jack Drago prompted.

She drew rein, and when she faced Drago it was with eyes full of concern. 'You'd need to have a hole in your head to stay in this valley, Jack,' she pleaded. 'Don't you understand? Sam Skelton,' again she spoke of her father as if he were an absolute stranger, 'can't let you be. If he does, it might put the steel in other men's spines to do as you've done. Besides, come spring, the Skelton herd will need every blade of grass this valley can provide.'

She reached out, placing her hand over his.

'Be sensible, Jack. Ride on. There's plenty of other valleys.' Her eyes swept over the valley with loving tenderness. 'Not as good, sure enough. But peaceful and almost as yielding.'

When she looked back to Jack Drago, and saw the determined slant of his jaw and the fiery resistance in his slate-grey eyes, Beth Crofton became angry.

'Do as you want,' she snapped. 'But you'll not see another spring!'

She urged the stallion she was on board to a canter, leaving Drago trailing her. He let her have her space. Beth Crofton was not a woman to be

24

crowded anyway, he reckoned. They rode across the land he was determined to make his.

When Art Leary had dreamed around the thousand-and-one campfires they had shared over the years cow-punching for the Double R, Drago had indulged the Irishman's colourful description of the country he now found himself in, as whimsical and fanciful. But, as he had found out, Art Leary had not been dreaming. This valley was beyond a man's dreaming. As Beth had warned, he might never get to putting down roots here. But it was a place worth fighting for.

And he'd damn well fight to his last breath for it!

TWO

Sam Skelton stormed from the Bent Bough ranch house to watch Rick and Jake Barrett limp home.

'What happened?' His snarling question was addressed to Rawlson. 'You seem to be scratch-free, Ned?' he observed shrewdly.

'That's 'cause he stood by and did nothing to help, Pa,' Rick Skelton groused.

'A stranger, Mr Skelton,' Jake lied. 'Got the drop on us.'

'Got the drop on you, huh?' the Bent Bough boss quizzed Jake, not duped for a second by this untruth. 'Three of you – one of him? Doesn't seem the kind of odds a stranger would buck?'

'Jake's telling it like it happened, Pa,' Rick Skelton said, backing Jake Barrett's lie. 'Come right outa nowhere down at Brown's Creek.'

The rancher's questioning eyes went to Ned Rawlson.

'That the way it happened, Ned?'

Rawlson, who had come to the valley with Sam Skelton, had failed through a series of misfortunes and bad luck to make the kind of impact the Bent Bough owner had made. He had finally settled for a monthly wage as Sam Skelton's ramrod and sometimes enforcer, (though the latter was a task he did not relish) after his wife had fallen from a buckboard and broken her neck and his spirit.

He did not like the idea of backing Rick and Jake Barrett's tall tale, but there was little else he could do. Drawing Rick Skelton's spite on his head was not something any sane man would do.

'That's the gist of it, Sam.'

Not fully convinced of the tale's veracity, Sam Skelton still accepted it. Because if he did not, it would mean that there was a stranger in the valley, who had sent the trio packing, Rick and Jake the worse for wear. A stranger of such calibre meant trouble, and trouble he was tiring of. The Cattlemen's Association was considering him as their candidate for political office in the spring election, and Skelton considered that Washington office was a plum worth plucking. Besides, of late, he had lost his appetite for the continuous wrangling that fighting off each new claim for the valley's free range embroiled him in. Maybe the years were piling up faster than he'd like to admit. He'd come round to thinking a lot about his late wife, and his daughter Beth's ostracization, and the injustice he'd done both women. Whatever was motivating his softening attitude to strangers putting down roots in Tomb Valley, there was no denying that it was there.

'Saw him ride off with Beth, Pa,' Rick snarled. 'Real cosy they were, too.'

'She help him?' the rancher growled.

'Help,' Barrett griped. 'Why, she took his part by not sidin' with us.'

Ned Rawlson did not put up any defence against this point of view. It proved to be a wise decision, as Sam agreed with Barrett's opinion.

'We should run Beth and that no-good husband of hers right off the range, Pa,' Rick fumed.

'She's kin,' the rancher said.

Rick Skelton scoffed. 'Then why ain't she right here, Pa? And why is she always ready to offer support to everyone who bucks you?'

'Beth's like her ma,' Sam Skelton flung back. 'Ready to help any lame dog that comes along.'

'Beth's either with us or against us, Pa,' Rick Skelton raged. 'That's the way I see it.'

'Hands off Beth!' Sam Skelton dictated. 'Some day that gal will get sense and come home. I'll put my bottom dollar on that happening.'

Beth coming home was what worried Rick most, with Sam Skelton in the kind of reminiscing and placatory mood he'd been in of late.

28

'Meantime, you're going to let her give comfort to those who'd rob you of the valley, Pa?' he said sneakily.

'As I see it,' Sam said, 'all this stranger's done was give you boys a hard time, which,' his tone became granite hard, 'with the odds he was bucking is to your shame.'

'He's trouble, Pa,' the rancher's son predicted. 'I just know he is. Ain't that so?' he asked the others.

Sam Skelton looked to Rawlson for confirmation of Rick's assessment. Rawlson's reply was an honest one.

'I reckon he might be at that, Sam.'

'What signs did you see that that might be the case, Ned? Mightn't this fella be like all the others, easily scared?'

Rawlson opined: 'Don't think so. Got a nester's look 'bout him, Sam. Lord knows we've seen off enough in our time to recognize their kind.'

The rancher scoffed. 'No one's that loco. There's hardly a corner of Wyoming left where word hasn't reached about the effect of settling in Tomb Valley has on a man's health.'

'Some men don't listen good, Sam,' Rawlson said. 'And more don't listen at all.'

'The stranger's trouble, Pa,' Rick Skelton repeated. 'Best if we put a spoke in his plans right now, before he gets to thinking we ain't got the grit to do it.'

29

''Ned?' Sam grunted.

Rawlson had an admiration for Jack Drago's courage. Over the years the Skelton crews had put rabbit-fast legs under anyone who had the gumption or crass stupidity to lay claim to a sod of what Sam Skelton considered his domain. But this man was different from the usual run-of-the-mill hobo who had entertained notions of nesting. He had about him an air of successfully staking his claim, or dying in the process of trying.

He had watched him ride off with Beth Crofton, and they looked as natural together as peas in a pod – him with the virility in his loins of a mountain cat, and Beth with the hips to produce the fruit of those loins. They were a pair made for each other, of that he was sure. They had sparked, and, Rawlson reckoned, the flame from that spark might not be easily extinguished. Beth had stood by Ben Crofton because she was the kind of woman who, once committed, saw her task through. But Crofton was not the man for her. It was no secret that when her ma died, Beth had married the lay-about simply as an act of defiance of Sam, and to be free of him and Rick. She had remained childless, except for a scare early on when she had lost a baby. No one blamed Beth for that. Folk had placed the blame squarely on weak seed.

Ned Rawlson worried about Beth, whom he had

seen grow from nipper to woman. Sam Skelton would chew the cud with her endlessly, but he would never harm her, of that he was certain. Of one other thing he was also certain. If Sam or Rick tried, he'd kill them. Beth's only sin in Sam's eyes was being born a girl. Rick Skelton would never have been born if Beth had been a boy, and Sam Skelton would never have wandered off the way he had. But life did not always run in straight lines.

Rawlson's worry extended to the time beyond Sam Skelton, when the bad-tempered Rick would be boss of the Bent Bough ranch. He'd not show the same tolerance of Beth which Sam had. Sam could not last for ever. His visits to Doc Crowe's office had become more frequent, and his colour had, in recent months, become ruddier. And there were those persistent rumours about him seeking political office. Washington was a long way off, and if Sam went there he might as well be on the moon. Rick would have a free hand, which would not augur well for Beth. And if the stranger were still around, which was unlikely, he'd swing from the nearest tree.

Maybe it would be best to deal with the stranger now? For his and Beth's sake. Because they were too easy in each other's company for trouble to be avoided, and not the kind of trouble that was currently under discussion.

Why he should care about what happened to the stranger was a mystery to Rawlson. He owed him nothing. But there was no denying the feeling that in the stranger, a man had finally come to Tomb Valley who just might make a difference to the way things were done.

Many times he had wished that someone would stand up to Sam Skelton. He could not help but think that if they had, Beth would still be at home or, if married, she'd be wed to a man like the stranger and not the weakling Crofton. Ellie Skelton might still be alive, too. And Sam might have been a different man, if on those first skirmishes a man had happened along who would have stood against him....

A man like the stranger.

Was it too late for change? Sam had made mutterings to him about change, but he couldn't see Rick changing his spots. If he were to tell Sam to let the stranger be, would he eventually bring about Drago's demise? Maybe it would be best for him to take a beating and be run out. Maybe, Rawlson thought, Beth would have enough sense to leave with him. With weary resignation, he answered Sam Skelton's question.

'I guess spoking his plans would be wisest, Sam.'

A way on, her anger spent, Beth Crofton drew rein

in a shady dell. Drago took his sweet time in closing the distance between them, figuring that Beth would not have much appreciation of a lapdog approach. Besides, she needed to be taught that Jack Drago was not a man who would necessarily come every time she beckoned. When he ambled up to where she was and dismounted, he could see a glint of humour in her eyes.

'I guess if I was standing here buck-naked and craving, you'd have not put one foot faster past the other, would you, Jack?' Beth said.

He laughed. 'If you'd care to test that theory, ma'am?'

They laughed together, easy and slow, the way old friends do. In the quiet lull that followed, Jack Drago had his thoughts, as he was sure Beth Crofton had hers, some of which were scarlet. But most of which were regretful that he had not met Beth before she had tied herself to another man.

In the short time since he had met Beth Crofton, he had lost some of his resolve to settle in the valley, and not because of any fear of what her father might do. His budding change of heart sprang from another fear, a fear which he had had little experience in dealing with – the fear of what this woman might come to mean to him. Land he could claim and fight for, and would. It was his right. But another man's wife was not his right, and he knew that already he was smitten with

Beth Crofton, and if he was reading the signals correctly, though he'd not claim any expertise, she, too, had a hankering for him.

Some kindlings took time to flourish. Others, he now knew, took no time at all.

She huddled against the first flakes of snow sweeping off the mountains, driven by a biting wind that had been building from a breeze for the last fifteen minutes, or so. She pulled the long coat she wore more tightly around her, and the outline of her figure sharpened. Drago's heart leapt along with other parts. Instinctively, because it seemed the right thing to do, though Jack Drago could not come up with a single reason why it should be, he put his arm around her shoulders. Beth snuggled against him with a familiar ease that was much older than the time they'd been together. There wouldn't be a chance in hell that any watcher would think that this was the very first time that Beth Crofton was in Jack Drago's arms.

Beth's smile was one of impish mischief.

'Folk might say that you've taken a liberty, Jack Drago!'

Jack Drago's returning smile was vagabondly wry.

'Well, now, it's only a liberty if the lady objects, I reckon.' His gaze held hers. 'Are you objecting, Beth?'

A frown puckered her brow. 'I should be, Jack.' She nestled against him and murmured, 'I surely should be.'

THREE

'If you ever reach Abbot Creek,' Art Leary had said to Jack Drago at their last camp-fire, the night before they drove their last herd into Abilene, 'you be sure to look up a fella by the name of Nate Haskin. Him and me shared a poker table for a whole week one snowy winter, until he cleaned me out.'

Leary had laughed, his trail-dust reddened eyes full of what were clearly fond memories.

'Had to give me lodgin's in the town jail 'til I got a poke together again by doin' most jobs 'round Abbot Creek that no one else would do.'

'I'll give him a holler if he's still sucking air,' Drago had promised. 'I take it, if he gave you lodgings in the town pokey, Nate Haskin is the badge-toter in Abbot Creek, Art?'

Art Leary had rubbed his cheek in remembrance.

'Packs a hammer right mitt. Drove me 'most clear to hell.'

Drago had laughed.

'Looks like you and this Haskin fella were bosom buddies, by the way you're remembering him?'

'Yes, we were, Jack. But bein' friends with that old bastard would never stop him landin' a brain-shaker on ya, if the occasion called for it.'

He had confided: 'One night I hung on the mother of all booze-ups. Drank Kentucky rye. Got kinda tetchy. Rye – particularly Kentucky rye – since I wore Union blue, never did settle well with me.

'Well, just as I was about to face up to a gambler who was as gun-slick as a rattler is mean, in walks Nate Haskin to the Silver Mustang saloon.'

He spoke in a different voice, presumably Nate Haskin's. And if it was, Drago thought amusedly, the Abbot Creek lawman ate nails for breakfast.

' "Leary", he says to me, with a face that would put the run on Satan. "You go for that gun and I'll whup you like you've never been whupped before".' Art Leary's toothless laughter had had most of the Double R crew laughing that night, so infectious had it been. 'Told the silk-vested gambler the same.'

His laughter had gone up a notch, and was whining enough to scare away a mountain cat who had been worrying the camp.

'Diff'rence was,' Leary rubbed his chin again,

'the gambler had the smarts to take heed. Me, I bucked Haskin and got a pile-driver that near drove me right through the rear wall of the Silver Mustang. And I tell ya straight, Jack. If that wall hadn't held, why, shit, I'd have ended up in Mexico.

'So, like I said. If you ever set foot in Abbot Creek, and Haskin's still 'bove ground, you tell him that Art Leary sends his best.'

On the promise that he would, they had turned in that night, Drago never figuring that it would be the last night that they would do so together.

Sam Skelton, not a man to dally once he made up his mind, ordered a horse to be saddled.

'Best send this stranger packing right now, I guess,' he told Rick and Ned Rawlson. He instructed another ranch hand to ride to Abbot Creek. 'Fetch Doc Crowe 'long to see Jake. Tell Nate Haskin that I want no interference from the law.' His next pronouncement was grim. 'I'll attend to this damn stranger alone. The stranger is on Skelton range, and that means Skelton justice applies. Which,' he railed, 'will be fast and final, if he doesn't make tracks out of the valley, pronto.'

Jack Drago held Beth Crofton in his arms for a long, silent time, neither seeming in a hurry to resume their journey to the Crofton place. The snow had thickened and the temperature had dropped by the second, but it did not seem to matter.

Conscious of facing Ben Crofton, Drago was thinking of heading for town. Having held Crofton's wife in his arms, and having committed mortal sin in his soul with her, as he expected she had with him, he doubted very much if Crofton would be fooled. The kind of minutes they had shared together would glow in them for a long time.

His desire for Beth Crofton was coal-hot. But it wasn't only desire. He had desired and bedded many women during his years on the cow-trails. The feelings he had for Beth were different, yet the same.

Beth was not a woman to be taken like other women, and he would not want to do so. Jack Drago knew that once he tasted Beth Crofton's pleasures, he sure as hell wouldn't want to leave. He had avoided a woman's leash since the first man's hair had sprouted on his chin, enjoying and experiencing their delights, but never taking one on board. He had never thought he would, until he held Beth Crofton in his arms. Now he was a man ready for a leash. The only problem was, Beth Crofton wasn't free to sling that leash on him. She was another man's woman and he had no rights, other than those of a vagabond, should Beth Crofton be willing to take him to her bed. If that were the case he'd not say no; he wasn't that strong. But Drago knew that should that happen, he'd leave Beth Crofton's bed a sickened man, pining for the rest of his days for a woman whom, he now believed, even after their short acquaintance, was his natural soul mate.

The sighing wind that blew ghostily through the shady dell in which they'd stopped was as desolate as the caverns of Jack Drago's heart.

'It might be best if I headed for town, Beth,' he said.

'Maybe,' she replied, her voice a hoarse whisper. 'Trails vanish fast in snow.'

Drago took her statement to mean that the sooner he left the better it would be. That was a fact, but it still stung Drago to think that she could be so practical, at a moment when good sense should be in short supply.

'Looks that way.'

'A stranger could get lost. Wander.'

'You reckon?'

'It's happened.'

'Guess I'd better make tracks, then.'

'I guess.'

They both knew that facing Ben Crofton together, they could not hide for long the glow they sparked in each other.

Reluctantly, and it pleased him to see the same reluctance in Beth, Drago released her from his arms and mounted his horse. He rode away, not daring to look back, lest he lose his resolve to not steal another man's wife.

When he crossed the creek beyond the dell, Beth would be out of sight, but his determination not to look back melted like a snowflake on hell's hobs. He turned in his saddle, already trying to strike a bargain with his Maker for what he was about to do. But Beth Crofton had vanished. His eyes searched the snowy landscape, and found no sign of her. She had gone up the opposite side of the dell, playing safe, out of sight to him.

The fact that Beth had chosen the trail she had, indicated that she, too, had tussled with her conscience. There was some consolation in that, he supposed. But Jack Drago's smile was a sad one.

'Hell,' he muttered. 'I'd rather have the prize than the damn glory!'

FOUR

'Where is he, Beth?' Sam Skelton demanded angrily of his daughter, storming from the house to meet Rick and Ned Rawlson, who had fruit-lessly searched the outbuildings of the meagre and ramshackle Crofton holding.

'Who the hell's Sam looking for?' Ben Crofton snapped at his wife, when his anger should have been directed at his father-in-law for his brash search of the house and his mean-tempered visit.

Beth Crofton had long ago given up on her husband standing up to Skelton's bullying. In fact she had long ago given up on Ben Crofton stand-ing up to any man. He was one of life's natural cringers. She now looked with distaste at the snivelling lapdog she shared her house and bed with, and wondered how, even to get out from under her father's tyranny, she had married a man as weak-minded and weak-willed as Ben Crofton.

'Beth,' he screamed at her. 'What man?'

Sam Skelton said: 'A stranger to the valley, Ben. Intent on trouble.'

Beth said: 'He didn't start the trouble, Father. Rick did.'

Sam Skelton swung around on her, eyes glittering with anger. Beth steadfastly refused to cower under her father's malevolent glare.

'Looks like you could have helped your brother, Beth,' the rancher fumed.

'Rick is not my brother,' Beth replied stonily.

'He's of my loins, just like you,' Sam Skelton stated unambiguously. 'In my book that makes Rick your brother.'

'What would you have me do, Father? Act like a Skelton, maybe? Fix every problem with a gun, a boot, or a rope?'

Sam Skelton raised his hand.

'You strike me,' Beth warned, 'and God help me, I'll curse you to Hell.'

Skelton stayed his hand.

'There were three Skelton men lined up against Jack Drago,' Beth said contemptuously. 'I didn't figure that they'd need any help dealing with one man.'

Skelton swung around on Ned Rawlson and Rick Skelton.

'The stranger got the drop on you, huh?'

'Drago wasn't looking for trouble, Father,' Beth

said. 'He stopped to enjoy the water of the creek and fill his canteen, that's all.'

'He's ridden on?' Sam Skelton quizzed Beth.

'No. He aims to settle in Tomb Valley.'

Ben Crofton stepped in. 'Settle? This is Skelton range, Beth.'

'You got that right, Ben,' his father-in-law growled. 'Settle where?' he asked Beth.

'Over near Mercer Falls.'

'That's range I'll be needing come spring. It's got good grass.'

'It's free range, Father,' Beth said, giving her father a reminder he did not need to hear. 'If Jack wants to claim it, he can.'

'Jack, huh?' Sam shot Ben Crofton a taunting leer. 'Seems to me, Beth, that you and Drago got to cosying up to each other really quick?'

Unintimidated by Crofton's poisonous glare, Beth said: 'Jack Drago is an easy man to get to know.'

Spitefully, her father raised his son-in-law's hackles.

'Seems to me, Ben, that you ain't giving your wife the attention she needs. If she takes up with a man who's only set foot in the valley.'

Beth, painfully aware of the trouble that her father's snide remarks were building up for her, said: 'We talked, that's all.'

But it had not been all. Nothing had happened

between Jack Drago and her, at least nothing tangible. But Beth was honest enough to admit that had Drago given vent to his desires, she would likely have been a willing partner in fornication. Maybe some shred of conscience would have kicked in, but considering the fire that still raged inside her since he had held her in his arms, Beth figured that even that shred of conscience would have vanished, had Jack Drago put his cards on the table.

Of one thing Beth was absolutely certain. She despised Ben Crofton with a new and vibrant hatred. Her father, she pitied. Sam Skelton could have been a giant of a man, if he had not let his dark side rule him.

Spurred by revulsion, Beth unequivocally stated: 'This place doesn't amount to much, Father. But what there is of it, is Crofton. So I'd appreciate it if you *gentlemen* left. Right now.'

Sam Skelton's rage purpled his face.

'You're ordering your own father off?' he croaked, his throat muscles constricted by his fury.

'Yes,' Beth said calmly.

He turned on Crofton. 'That your wish too, Ben?'

'Heck, Sam,' Crofton grovelled, 'you ain't takin' no heed of what a *woman* says, are ya?'

Skelton glowered. 'Seems to me Beth's wearing the pants 'round here, Ben.'

'Ain't so!' Crofton raged.

'In that case, I figure I'll stay a spell. Don't get to visit very often these days.'

Crofton fled ahead of Skelton to the house. 'Mighty glad to have you and your men, Sam. Got me some real fine malt—'

'That you ain't guzzled yet,' Sam mocked. 'Why, it must have just arrived before us, fellas,' he joked with Rawlson and Rick. 'A bottle don't stay long on the shelf at all with Ben.'

For a fleeting second, Beth felt pity for her wastrel husband, as the pain of hurt caused by her father's cruel words showed in his washed-out eyes. She might have respected him some, had he given free rein to the momentary glint of anger that flashed in his eyes after her father's demeaning jibes. But Ben Crofton was a man too used to living without pride; and pride had become too distant a goal to achieve again.

'Ain't that a fact, Sam,' Crofton laughed, prancing about like one of the red-nosed clowns one saw in the travelling shows that visited Abbot Creek from time to time.

'There's no hospitality here for you, Father,' Beth reiterated. Skelton swung around. Beth ate up his scowling glare. 'Not until you visit as a father should.'

'Don't you pay no heed, Sam,' Crofton whined. 'Beth's just upset that you want to run this fella

46

Drago outa the valley. She always did have a soft spot for strays.'

'Jack Drago is no stray,' Beth stated. 'In fact, Father, Jack Drago might just be the man who'll stand against the Bent Bough.'

'Then he won't be standing for long,' Rick Skelton screamed.

'Rick is right, Beth,' Sam Skelton said. He swung on to his horse. 'So my advice to you is to give this Drago *hombre* a wide berth. There's bound to be a lot of lead-filled air around him, if he doesn't see sense and ride on.'

Sam Skelton thundered out of the Crofton yard, with Rick Skelton hard pressed to keep pace. Ned Rawlson lingered for a moment to offer some advice.

'It would be best if you used your influence with Drago to ride on, Beth,' he said.

Beth smiled kindly on Rawlson, having fond memories of how he and his wife Mary had been her mother's only friends in her darkest days with Sam Skelton.

'Why does a decent man like you stay around men like my father and Rick, Ned?'

Rawlson shrugged. 'Sometimes, Beth, a man hasn't got the choosing. This valley is where my best memories are. And where Mary is resting.'

Their dust dispersing, Ben Crofton bore down on his wife, face livid, fists balled. Beth drew the

47

rifle from her saddle scabbard and held it unwaveringly on her husband.

'Come a step closer, Ben, and so God help me, I'll plant you,' she promised.

His rat's eyes studied Beth, and concluding that she meant what she said, he effortlessly slid back into grovelling.

'It ain't right that we should be quarrellin',' Beth. Now, put down that rifle and come inside the house.' He grinned leerily. 'We ain't been *close* for a long while.'

Beth held the Winchester steady. 'From now on you stay out of my bed, Ben,' she ordered.

'You're talkin' crazy, Beth.' A snarl twisted his face. 'We're man and wife. There ain't no sep'rate beds for us, you hear?'

Beth Crofton snorted. 'Some marriages are made in heaven, Ben – some in hell. It isn't hard to see where ours was thought up.'

Crofton flared. 'I reckon your pa got it right when he as good as said that you and this fella Drago got real pally, Beth?'

'Father was giving free rein to his spiteful nature, Ben,' Beth told her husband. 'Nothing happened between Jack Drago and me.'

'Not 'cause you didn't want it to, Beth!' Crofton observed perceptively.

'I guess there might just be a grain of truth in what you say, Ben,' Beth answered honestly.

'I'll kill the bastard!' Crofton swore.

'No you won't, Ben,' Beth said, sadly. 'You'll get drunk. That's what you'll do.'

He shook his head vehemently.

'Don't try, Ben,' Beth cautioned her husband. 'Drago will kill you.'

He scoffed. 'It'd be mighty convenient making you a widder, wouldn't it?'

Beth relaxed. Ben Crofton had found an excuse for not acting as a man should on getting an admission from his wife of her desire for another man. He shuffled towards the house, licking dry lips, headed for the new batch of malt he'd brought home from Abbot Creek a couple of days previously.

Beth watched him, skinny shoulders hunched, whipped and sorry for himself, and her anger evaporated. She thought that it might be a kindness if he got the spit to challenge Jack Drago. Drago would most assuredly kill him. But in death Ben Crofton might find some pride.

Before he had gone far the snow had thickened to the point where Drago could barely see his own hand. Trails which had been clear-cut only ten minutes previously had been secreted away under the snow, and the terrain had a sameness that lured the traveller on to strange paths, which often wound back to where a man had started out from.

49

Being a much-travelled man, Jack Drago knew that the snowy landscape held unseen dangers that could ensnare a man and leave him helpless. A snapped horse-leg was one such danger, and probably the greatest, too. Without a horse, in unknown country, with temperatures plummeting, in snow-soaked clothing, a man would not last long.

Abbot Creek was only ten miles distant. But, even knowing the way, ten miles in such weather was a long way. And if he took a wrong direction there was a snowy vastness beyond Abbot Creek in which a man could wander until death kindly took him.

Beyond the valley it was flat, featureless country, devoid of landmarks, country full of potential and deadly pitfalls. Drago reckoned that he was about half-way between Crofton's place and town, where turning back or going forward had as much for or against a change of direction.

Having spent over ten years driving Texas steers, Drago was used to sun on his skin and heat in his bones, therefore the effects of the intense and bitterly seeping chill of the snowstorm was greatly magnified, and would drain his energy quickly.

His preoccupation with the weather and its sapping effect, took second place to the sudden appearance of three men in the snow ahead. They weren't near enough for him to definitely recognize them, but their searching ride told him that he was again about to cross paths with the Skelton outfit.

The trio's leader was bulky in the saddle, having the beef on him of an older man – Sam Skelton? The long-limbed skinny rider alongside him, Drago recognized as Rick Skelton. The third man, he guessed to be the older and more reasonably minded of the trio he'd tangled with at Brown's Creek.

A sudden gust of wind served the searchers and the sought with equal fairness. As Drago caught sight of them, so they saw him. The gap in the blizzard closed as swiftly as it had opened. Maybe, Drago hoped, their paths might not cross, but that was unlikely. The Skeltons would know every inch of the valley, whereas he knew nothing of it. Resignedly, Jack Drago knew that there was trouble looming.

Big and ugly trouble.

FIVE

Drago was no fool. The odds were stacked against him. Three to one were not odds a wise man engaged with. Sam and Rick Skelton were used to seeing men run with their tails between their legs when the Bent Bough crew showed up. The last thing they'd have expected was to come across a man who did not run easily. Back at the creek, surprise had favoured him. But now he was a known quantity.

This time the Skeltons would be ready.

The blizzard would cover him for a time. With luck, the heavily falling snow would quickly obliterate his tracks. But he'd need the devil's own luck for it to hold all the way to Abbot Creek, if in fact that was the direction he was headed in. He could equally be riding into a Skelton trap.

Jack Drago's luck ran out. As quickly as it had thickened, the blizzard thinned. It took no time at all for the Bent Bough riders to get a bead on him.

They veered in his direction; their strong, well-fed, well-muscled horses eating up the ground. His slack-sided mount, having covered a long trail and hard miles was no match. Though she was willing, sensing the danger coming her way, Drago calmed the mare, seeing no point in punishing the horse for nothing. Drago stood his ground, and waited for the riders to reach him. Sam Skelton brought his fine stallion nose to nose with Drago's scrawny mare.

'This the fella who gave you sissies a hard time?' he growled at Rick and Ned Rawlson. 'Doesn't look much in the way of trouble to me.'

Drago said: 'I didn't start trouble. Neither am I looking for any.'

'If you just keep riding, there won't be any,' Sam Skelton said.

'I gotta score to even, Pa,' Rick griped.

'It'll be settled,' the Bent Bough boss promised. 'Then,' he addressed Drago, 'if you've got sense, that'll be an end of this.'

The rancher's angry eyes locked with Drago's. 'Take your punishment. Then get out.'

'The northern end of this valley is open range, Skelton,' Drago said. 'I aim to claim a slice of that range.'

'See, Pa,' Rick Skelton raged. 'Told you he's looking for trouble.' His pistol flashed in his hand. 'Let me plant him now, and he ain't going to be no more trouble.'

'My boy's reasoning makes for good sense, mister,' Skelton senior said. 'Any reason you can give me why I shouldn't take it?'

'One good reason.'

'And that would be?'

'I reckon that I'm fast enough to get off a shot before I go down.' Drago's glance, colder than the landscape they parleyed in, went Rick Skelton's way. 'And I'm counting on that bullet finding your boy's heart.'

Rick Skelton snorted. 'My gun is cocked, fool. There's no way you'll clear leather before I plug you.'

Drago addressed Sam Skelton. 'I've got to admit that the odds favour your boy, Skelton. The thing is, are you willing to play those odds?'

Sam Skelton looked deeply into Jack Drago's eyes, trying to read his mind. Drago's slate-grey eyes remained coldly blank. He had decided that he was staying in the valley, alive or dead. He had spent too many years eating dirt on cattle drives and dossing down in squalid bunkhouses, to want to take up that way of life again. Art Leary had handed him a dream, and he had decided over the months it had taken him to reach Tomb Valley that he was going to make it come true, or die in the attempt.

'I can take him, Pa,' Rick Skelton said, with the cockiness of a fool.

'Your years are counting down, Skelton,' Drago said to Sam. 'You've only got one boy to hand your kingdom on to ... Of course, there's always Beth.'

'A woman is good for babies and keeping a man's house, and that's about it,' the rancher growled. 'A ranch needs a man's hand.'

Drago glanced Rick Skelton's way.

'Then, I guess dead or alive, you've got real problems, Skelton.'

Incensed, Rick Skelton raised his gun. Drago, with the speed of a mountain cat threw himself from his horse. Skelton's bullet whined harmlessly past. Before he hit the soft snow, Drago's Colt .45 was in his hand and spitting. His bullet, kept intentionally high and wide, grazed Rick Skelton's neck, and took the lobe of his right ear with it as it skewered away. The rancher's son howled. Drago's next bullet whipped the gun from his hand. Sam Skelton's Peacemaker cleared leather and swung Drago's way. Drago knew he had run out of time....

And luck.

A second gun spoke – a Winchester. Beth Crofton stepped from behind a pair of pines growing out of each other, about thirty feet distant.

'Enough!' Beth ordered. 'All round.'

'You're saving this bastard's skin, you bitch,' Rick screamed.

'Drago could have killed you, Rick,' Beth said.

'You know that, Father. Rick started this. So I say you call it quits now.'

'Just like your ma,' Sam Skelton raged. 'Always helping lame dogs at the expense of your own kind. I should have drowned you the day you were born, gal.'

Beth sighed. 'Maybe that would have been best all round, Father.'

'Get out of the valley and stay out,' the Bent Bough owner told Drago. 'Maybe next time you won't have a skirt to hide behind.'

'I'm beholden,' Drago thanked Beth. 'But I'd appreciate it if you bowed out.' To Sam Skelton, he said: 'I'm not leaving, and I'm not hiding. If you want to settle this right now ...'

'Is that the way you want it, Father?' Beth asked.

Sam Skelton took a moment to consider his options. Thinking about the bleak future which Drago had painted for the Bent Bough ranch without a son to pass it on to, he chose to let matters be.

'Let's make tracks for now,' he told Rick and Ned Rawlson.

'But, Pa,' Rick Skelton whined.

'Shut your mouth,' Skelton senior flung back. 'Ride!'

Jack Drago watched the trio disappear in the again thickening snow.

'Drago,' Beth said, 'either you're a man who won't be pushed, or you're a fool who doesn't know when to quit. Either way you're trouble. Do as my father says. Ride on.'

She turned to leave. Drago grabbed her by the arm, swinging her back against him, where he held her tightly despite her attempts to break free.

'Beth Crofton,' he said. 'I told your stubborn mule of an old man, and now I'm telling you. I'm settling in this valley. You Skeltons can take it or leave it, lump it or like it. But I'm staying.'

He kissed her with a raw passion that left them both fighting for breath. Then he released his hold on her, casting her aside. He mounted up and rode away.

'If it's Abbot Creek you're seeking,' she called. He drew rein. 'Ride in a straight line, due south.' Without another word Beth Crofton turned and strode back through the deep snow to where she had hitched her horse. She mounted up and rode into a stretch of pine. A little way on, on a rise of ground, she drew rein and watched Jack Drago's departing figure. Her emotions overwhelmed her and she wept.

'Damn it, Jack Drago,' she murmured weepily, 'why did you ever come to Tomb Valley?'

SIX

Marshal Nate Haskin opened one rheumy eye to look at the visitor coming through the law-office door, gauging in a second flat the threat or lack of it from the tall, six-foot stranger. He eased back on the hammer of the .45 he had hidden under the blanket that covered him on the horsehair couch on which he took his siesta. Not a young man any more, the 6 a.m. start took its toll on his energy in the afternoon, particularly on the day he partook of the fare in the Silver Fork café – Mollie Ambrose sent a man away satisfied. Her stew, each over-loaded plate of it, seldom left a vacant chair.

'Marshal Haskin?' Drago enquired.

'Who's asking?' the lawman mumbled, not bothering to hide his displeasure at having his nap interrupted.

'Name's Jack Drago, Marshal.'

'Been expecting you.'

The lawman's tone was unfriendly.

'Word travels fast in there parts.'

'Faster than the wind,' Haskin said tersely.

Drago did not take offence at the lawman's lack of welcome. He understood how thorny a man could get when his slumber was disturbed. In his time, he'd had his share of unwelcome intrusions, which had not settled well with him either. Recalling Art Leary's sketch of the crusty marshal, he grinned.

'Did I say something droll, mister?' Haskin asked, a touch testily.

'Art Leary said you were an ornery sort of cuss,' Drago said. Nate Haskin opened his second eye. 'He was right.'

'Art Leary, huh? You know that old bastard?'

'We were trail partners for almost ten years. Driving cattle to Abilene.'

Haskin smirked. 'I thought he'd be roasting in Hell by now, the old buzzard?'

'Maybe he is,' Drago said sombrely. 'But I reckon he's on harp duty.'

'Dead?'

Drago nodded.

'When?'

'A while back.'

'Where?' Haskin enquired.

'Abilene. A kid on a fast track to a reputation.'

Nate Haskin let out a weary sigh. 'Poker game, I guess?'

'You guessed right.'

'Couldn't play for fiddly. But had the devil's own luck. The kind that got men sour.'

'The kid wasn't interested in the pot. He liked killing.'

'Well, now that I'm awake,' the lawman swung his long legs off the couch, removed his hat and palmed his hairless dome, 'I might as well brew some Java.' He took in Drago's drenched and perished appearance. 'Laced with a dollop of whiskey, I reckon.'

'That would be welcome indeed, sir,' Drago said.

'Best shed those wet clothes, too,' Haskin advised. The lawman ran his eyes over his visitor's length. He went through to the cells and came back with a bundle of dry clothes. 'Should about fit.'

'Thank you, Marshal.'

'Don't thank me. Thank Matthew Brodin.'

'Matthew Brodin?'

'Hanged for murder only last week.'

Drago instantly dropped the clothes.

Haskin chuckled. 'He's dead. He won't be needing them any more. And if you don't get out of those wet duds, you'll likely be joining Brodin before long.'

'Guess you've got a point, Marshal.'

'If you're shy you can shuck your clothes in a cell.'

Drago laughed. 'I spent ten years in bunk-houses.'

'Then you ain't shy.'

While Haskin went about brewing Java, Drago changed his clothes. The marshal asked: 'What're you doing in Abbot Creek, Mr Drago?'

'Right now I'm saying hello for Art Leary.'

'A long way to come to say hello,' Haskin observed. He liberally laced the freshly brewed coffee with a decent bottle of whiskey. There's got to be more to your visit than that?'

He poured a cup of the steaming brew and handed it to Drago. Then he sat behind his desk and waited for his visitor to elaborate. Drago told Haskin about the thousand-and-one camp-fires he had shared with Art Leary, and about his friend's constant dreaming about the valley to the south of Abbot Creek.

'As close as you'll ever get to heaven, was how Art described the valley, Marshal. And he was right.'

'I guess that'd be Tomb Valley you're talking about,' Haskin said, and added a warning. 'That's Bent Bough range, Drago. Sam Skelton territory. And he doesn't take none too kindly to interlopers.'

Drago chuckled. 'So I've found out, Marshal.'

'You've exchanged, ah … *greetings* with Sam, I take it?'

'I have.'

'Then I reckon you know how Skelton feels about strangers putting down roots in Tomb Valley?'

'He didn't mince his words,' Drago confirmed. Then, resolutely, 'Neither did I.'

Nate Haskin supped his coffee for a long spell. 'Want some advice?' he asked.

'Depends.'

'Forget that old buzzard Leary ever mentioned Tomb Valley. That's if you've got sense inside that skull of yours, Drago.'

'And if I don't have sense? And I don't want to forget?' Jack Drago asked quietly.

'Then, Sam Skelton will kill you,' the lawman stated bluntly.

'Wouldn't you have something to say about that, Marshal?'

'You don't understand—'

'No. I don't,' Drago interjected, 'if you're saying that as marshal you'd stand by and let it happen.'

Haskin put down his tin cup. He reached behind to a shelf to grab two glasses. He half-filled the glasses with whiskey, and shoved one across the desk to Drago.

'Let me fill in the picture for you, Drago.' He slugged. 'Tomb Valley—'

'Is free range,' Drago interjected. 'At least the north end of the valley is.'

62

'Impatient fella, aren't you?'

'It's been said,' Drago murmured.

'Knew a lot of impatient men,' Haskin observed. 'All dead.'

The atmosphere between the men smouldered.

'You ready to listen?' the marshal asked.

'Figure I don't have a choice,' Drago growled, angered by what he saw as the lawman's reluctance to back his legitimate claim.

Haskin elaborated.

'Tomb Valley, as far back as folk can remember, has been Skelton range. And,' he stressed, 'Abbot Creek's a Skelton town.' The lawman took another long slug of whiskey, before continuing: 'This town is beholden to the Bent Bough for its continued existence, Drago. There isn't much else round here for folk to put bread on their tables from. We had a couple of mining hopes from time to time, but they amounted to nothing. Maybe,' he speculated, 'if they had ...' He shrugged. 'But they didn't. The Bent Bough hires almost fifty men, more come round-up. A whole lot of bellies would go slack without Skelton dollars to fill them.

'Here in town, Bent Bough dollars keep the stores' tills jangling, too. Simply put, Drago, this town doesn't care a fig about your claim for Tomb Valley range, free or not. You upset Sam Skelton, and they won't look on you none too kindly.'

'What kind of town is this?' Drago asked angrily.

Haskin shrugged. 'The kind of town that looks after its own first. Not unlike other towns, Drago.' The lawman sighed wearily. 'The fact is, that what Sam Skelton says, goes. And what Sam Skelton wants, he gets.'

'As the marshal you're duty bound to uphold the law, and defend my right to free range,' Drago said stubbornly.

'Well, now,' Nate Haskin drawled, 'the way I see it, my first duty is to keep trouble to a minimum for the good folk of Abbot Creek. And, while conceding your right to free range, siding with you against Sam Skelton ain't going to do that, mister,' the marshal finished, doggedly determined.

While understanding Haskin's reasoning, Jack Drago still fumed. 'Don't you ever get sick of kowtowing to Sam Skelton, Marshal?'

The marshal rose from his chair as if the world was on his two shoulders pressing him down.

'I know how this must look to you, Drago,' he barked. 'But I keep the peace in this town whatever way I can. You've got a right to stake your claim, but I've also got a duty to clear the decks and tell you how it's going to be, if you do.'

His features set in stone.

'Skelton will string you up, cut your throat, or

sink lead in you. Depends on how he feels on the day.' Haskin's face curled in distaste. 'If Rick Skelton gets his way, he'll probably haul you behind a buckboard 'til you're raw meat. Then he'll feed you to the dogs!'

He strode across the office to the window, his back rigid with anger. Briefly, a couple of riders going past got his attention. When he spoke, it was with the resigned tone of a man who had long ago shelved his pride, but had not liked doing so.

'If ...' He paused and changed tack, '*when*, Sam or Rick Skelton kills you, I could ride out to the Bent Bough, do a song and dance, haul one or both back here to the caboose.' He turned from the window, hopelessness pervading his faded blue eyes. 'I could send for a judge, arrange a trial, do all the paperwork that needs doing when a man is destined for a noose ...' The despair in his eyes changed to anger. 'But where the hell am I going to get a jury in this town to convict a Skelton of even breaking the most minor town law, let alone murder?

'Besides, Sam or Rick Skelton wouldn't be in jail long enough for a judge to arrive. The town would bust them out, even before his own men did. And if I stood in the way, Well ...'

Haskin's weariness and worry increased tenfold.

'I've got a wife, Drago – no kids. I don't aim to

make Alice a lonely widow, for a cause I damn well can't win.' Tiredly, he said: 'Ride on, Drago. Forget Tomb Valley.' He strode back across the office to face Drago and deliver a chilling warning. 'Unless you want to rest in it.'

Though angry as hell, Jack Drago had sympathy for the marshal. He reckoned that Art Leary had been right about Haskin being a good lawman. But it had been ten years since Art had been friends with Nate Haskin, and that span of time can make a whole lot of difference in a man's life. Haskin was older, close to handing in his badge and drawing on his pension, with a wife whom he clearly loved and fretted over. And he was standing alone in an owned town. Drago understood that such a combination of circumstances could take the steel from a man through fear, or by way of weary resignation to events. He wasn't the first lawman to lose hope in the face of insurmountable opposition.

From Jack Drago's point of view, the sad fact was, Nate Haskin was a lawman who had lost his grit. And that made him no help at all. He stood up to leave.

'You got a place to doss down?' Haskin asked. 'Money to pay for it?'

Drago's resources were meagre. No doubt Haskin had seen his lack of dollars in the ill-fitting and threadbare garb and scuffed boots he wore, his only half-respectable piece of clothing being his long bearskin coat.

'I was thinking about the livery, maybe?'

'Forget it,' Haskin said. 'Word of your ruckus with the Bent Bough will have reached town by now. Just saw a couple of Skelton punchers ride in. Eli Reilly, the livery owner, is a Christian and kindly man. He would probably feel that, as a Bible-abiding Christian, he'd be obliged to offer you shelter. But he'd only bring trouble on his own head, and he's not a young man.'

'Then I guess it'll have to be a derelict shack. Plenty of those in any town's backlots.'

Haskin scoffed. 'In this weather? Do that and you'll save Skelton having to hang you. I'm assuming, of course, that you're still intent on filing a claim for free range?'

'You're assuming correctly, Marshal,' Drago confirmed.

For the briefest of moments, there was a sparkle of remembered pride in the lawman's eye. 'I sure admire your gall, Drago,' he said.

Drago laughed easily. 'That could very well turn out to be my epitaph, I guess.'

Haskin laughed along with him. 'You know,' he said, his eyes wandering over Drago, 'this time Sam Skelton might just have bitten off more than he can comfortably chew.'

Drago was at the law-office door when Haskin

gave voice to the decision he'd been mulling over. He joined his visitor at the open door. He pointed along the street to a canary-yellow clapboard house at the end of the street that stood out in the grey, snowy landscape like a lantern above a whorehouse door.

'Alice likes bright colours,' Haskin explained. 'The sitting-room's got polka-dot wallpaper. Every time I see it my eyes pop.'

Drago tried to stifle his laughter, but failed.

'When you set eyes on it, you'll soon stop laughing. You'll be too damn busy wiping your watering eyes! You head along there now. Tell Alice I sent you, and that you need hot grub and a clean bed.'

Drago was knocked back on his heels by the marshal's generous offer.

'Won't Skelton take exception to you giving me room and board?' he worried.

'As sour as a darn lemon,' he said.

'I don't want to draw trouble on you and your wife's heads, Marshal.'

'That yellow clapboard doesn't amount to much, but it's mine and Alice's. We'll have whoever we feel like having under its roof,' Haskin declared spiritedly. 'And Sam Skelton can like it or lump it!'

'You have my thanks, Marshal.'

'Damn your thanks,' Haskin grumbled. 'I'd rather you'd mount up and ride on, Drago. But you ain't going to do that. So … Heck, git.'

'I don't aim to make trouble, Marshal,' Drago replied with equal candour. 'But if it comes, I'll not back away from it. I aim to put down roots in Tomb Valley, or be planted there if that's my Maker's will.'

Jack Drago spun around and headed towards the marshal's house. Not having put too many steps beyond the law office, he noted the drift of men from the Silver Mustang saloon up ahead. Two of the men Drago recognized as the riders who had got Haskin's attention a short time before as they rode past the law office. They straddled the boardwalk. If Drago wanted to pass, he would have to step off the walkway.

He wasn't going to.

A third man, clearly a backer, wore a thonged, low-slung Colt .45 sporting a liberally notched walnut handle. Drago concluded that the fancily dressed, dust-free honcho was no ranch hand. Eyeing the notches on the man's gun, Drago also concluded that he was a damn liar, or a gunfighter to be reckoned with. The man hung back, leaning against a support strut of the saloon overhang, a sneer on his lips. He leisurely rolled a smoke as Drago approached, like a man might do it he were settling down to watch a saloon show or a tent-troupe performance.

One of the men blocking the boardwalk stepped forward, a sneer on his wide mouth; a mouth that was not wide to nature's design, but had been reshaped by fists. His eyes were small and mean, and glittered with the rot-gut he had consumed.

'Why, fellas,' he swaggered rakishly, the way a coward does when the odds favour him, 'if it ain't that gent who figures Mr Skelton is goin' to roll over and let him put down roots in Bent Bough range.'

The second man blocking the boardwalk said: 'Must've rocks in his head, Benjy.' He turned to address the gunslinger who was contentedly blowing smoke, though Drago had no doubt that his casual pose hid a readiness to spring into action, should his services be required. 'Don't you reckon so, Spicer?'

Spicer?

The gunslinger's monicker struck a chord with Drago. He looked with renewed interest at the quirley-puffer. His face had aged: ridges and valleys burned into it by the dry, hot south-of-the-border sun and wind. But it was him all right – Spicer McCall, formerly the Reverend Jediah McCall. Before he learned that in the brutal and cruel West, a six-gun had a lot more power of persuasion than the Bible, and was infinitely superior for robbing banks.

Drago's mind went back to a New Mexico border town where he had worn a deputy's badge for a short spell. He had, in his time, done a whole variety of jobs to keep body and soul together, and being a lawman had just been one, a means to an end.

The bank at Apache Gulch was about as secure as water in a holed bucket, and it did not take any great effort for the Reverend McCall to rob it of its meagre resources. It had been robbed several times before it had come to McCall's turn. But, McCall, not being the kind of experienced *hombre* who usually lifted the bank's cash, had lost his nerve.

Lucy Breen, the town's dressmaker, had just dropped by to put the couple of dollars she had earned that day into her account. Shocked on seeing McCall, still in his preaching garb, holding a gun on the bank teller, she had screamed loud enough to wake the longest of the dead in the town cemetery.

McCall, unnerved by the dressmaker's screams, shot her right between the eyes. Then, from her dead grasp, he grabbed the couple of dollars and fled from the bank, shooting back into the building, shouting: 'The bank's being robbed!' cleverly giving the impression that the robbers were still inside.

In the ensuing confusion, before the scared teller summoned up enough courage to come out and relay the true sequence of events, McCall had slipped away. By the time folk got it into their heads that it was the preacher who had robbed the bank and murdered Lucy Breen, Spicer McCall had made tracks to the border by a pre-planned route, over trails that most white men gave a wide berth to, due to an Apache fondness for them as a quick exit to Mexico.

The men who formed the posse were no more fearful or braver than the next man. But, with renegade Indians scalp-hunting, they soon lost their appetite for the chase. Dan Bradley, the sheriff of Apache Gulch, and his deputy Jack Drago, had risked giving McCall chase right up to Mexican territory, but with hot words wafting back and forth across the Rio Grande between the US and Mex governments about incursions into Mex territory, Bradley figured it the wiser course to draw rein at the border. The fact that the Mexican government had said that they would shoot at any illegal *Americano* on sight was another, and probably the deciding, factor, in Dan Bradley's abandonment of the chase.

'Don't want to end up rottin' in no stinkin' Mex jail,' he told Drago. He'd paled. 'Or be buzzard meat.'

Jack Drago had been of the opinion that with sign showing McCall not far ahead, they should maybe risk Mexican wrath. Bradley had been blunt in his rejection of this idea.

'If you're goin' after that Bible-thumping

bastard,' he'd said, 'you hand over your badge right now. I don't want no grief 'bout my deputy stirrin' trouble with the Mexes. You cross into Mex territory, and you ride on as John Citizen, Drago.'

It was Bradley's uncompromising stance that had opened up a rift between him and the sheriff which saw them part company a month later, just when Drago had had a hankering to settle for a permanent badge.

No one ever knew how the devil had got into the Reverend McCall that day, but his bloody history after that indicated that the demon had come to stay.

'Maybe, Charlie, someone shot him in the head and his brain escaped,' Spicer McCall murmured in the languid tone that Drago remembered when he was not preaching hell-fire sermons, in reply to the Bent Bough puncher's snide question.

McCall's observation much amused the duo blocking Drago's path.

'I'm not prodding for trouble, gents,' Drago said.

'He don't want no trouble,' Charlie sniggered. 'You hear that, Benjy?' He closed the gap between him and Drago in four loping strides, coming face to face with him. So close in fact that his spittle spattered Drago. 'You got trouble the second you set foot in Tomb Valley, mister,' he declared hotly. 'And I reckon you earned a place in eternity when you locked horns with Rick Skelton.

'Best you decide what you want on your tomb-stone, if you ain't headin' straight for your nag and riding out.'

Drago scowled darkly. 'I don't know how many times I have to say this around here. But I'm not going anywhere. I aim to have my rightful share of Tomb Valley.'

'Measure him and we'll oblige, fellas,' Spicer McCall drawled.

Jack Drago locked eyes with the gunfighter. 'You're a long way from Apache Gulch, Reverend.'

'Reverend?' Benjy questioned McCall.

'I guess these days you only use the Good Book as a pillow,' Drago added.

'Did he say reverend?' Charlie repeated.

'It's a long story,' McCall growled.

Curiosity piqued, McCall dropped his smoke and crushed the quirley underfoot. He pushed the other two Skelton men aside and came to stand in front of Drago. Recognition sparked in his eyes.

'You know this trouble-stirrer intimate like, Spicer?' Benjy quizzed, suspicion narrowing his eyes.

'I know him.'

'From where?' The question this time was Charlie's.

'From a place called Apache Gulch,' McCall informed his partners.

'Never heard of it,' Charlie said.

McCall laughed harshly. 'No one has. Apache Gulch is a fly-trap on the Mex border. Mr Drago was a deputy sheriff there when I robbed the bank.'

'A lawman?' There was a shake in Charlie's voice. Killing a lawman, even a former one, brought big trouble. The kind that usually concluded at the end of a rope.

McCall explained. 'Drago handed in his badge in a fit of pique, because the soft-belly sheriff of Apache Gulch wouldn't let him run me down in Mexico. Spent the years since looking up the rear ends of cows on the cattle trails, I heard.'

Spicer McCall chuckled.

'You know, Drago. I was only a sniff ahead of you. My horse went lame. You'd have had me for sure, if you'd had the grit to keep up the chase.'

Was that what had happened all those years ago? Had he, as McCall said, lost his grit, and used Bradley's caution as an excuse to cover his own yellowness? Though he had harked back to it often, he could never be sure if that was what had happened. He had, at the time, pondered on a man being alone in territory peopled with bandits, Apaches, and Mex soldiers, all eager and willing to kill a man just for the momentary diversion from boredom that it would bring. But, in kinder moments to himself, Jack Drago liked to think that, seeing himself as a future lawman, he had decided to uphold that law and not intrude into Mexico.

There was little point in going over old ground. He'd never really know for sure.

'Never figured you as a sod-buster, Drago,' McCall said.

'A man sometimes returns to old ways,' Drago answered stonily. 'I grew up in Iowa. There wasn't much to do in Iowa, if you didn't turn the sod.'

'You two are gettin' real pally, ain't ya,' Charlie said.

Spicer McCall scoffed. 'Don't worry, Charlie. My loyalties are with Skelton.'

'Then I guess you'd best be sending this cur on his way. That's what Mr Skelton pays you for, McCall.'

McCall scowled, and cautioned his Bent Bough cohort. 'Don't push.'

By now several men in town clothes had come from the saloon to watch the confrontation. A big-bellied man with florid cheeks, wearing a derby stepped forward to address Drago.

'Wes Lane.,' he introduced himself, and emphasized it with no small degree of self-importance. 'That would be Judge Wes Lane. You are not welcome in our midst, sir. This is a peace-loving community. You'll find no succour here. Best you do as Sam Skelton wants before his patience runs out.'

Lane's comments earned a chorus of approval.

'You're just the man I wanted to see, Judge,' Drago said. He took a sheet of parchment from his coat pocket with a rough pencil sketch on it. 'This here is a map of the free range I want to lay claim to in Tomb Valley. I'd be obliged if you'd make it legal.'

Lane was at first stunned, and then toweringly angry. 'Have you not listened to a word I've said, sir? Marshal,' he summoned Haskin.

Nate Haskin who had been watching the board-walk impasse, strolled along from the law office.

'Escort this man out of town, Marshal Haskin,' Lane ordered.

'Well, now, Judge,' Haskin said in a muted tone, 'I can't legally do that.'

'Can't do that?' Lane spluttered.

'No, sir,' Haskin said. 'Mr Drago ain't broken any laws that I know of.'

'I reckon that upsetting Sam Skelton is a good enough reason,' Lane ranted.

The crowd's approval of Lane's view was unstinting.

'Good reasons and legal reasons ain't the same, Judge,' Haskin said. 'Being a judge, you should know that.'

'Are you taking Drago's side against Mr Skelton, Marshal?' McCall asked with quiet menace.

Haskin's dislike for the gunfighter showed on his face, as clear as a lamp down a coal mine.

'Good question, Nate,' Lane said.

Haskin said stoutly, 'Ain't a matter of sides. It's a matter of right and wrong.'

The marshal's stand came as a surprise to Drago, and even more of a surprise to his fellow citizens. Lane reacted angrily.

'Tomb Valley is Skelton range,' he declared. 'Every damn blade of grass in it!'

'I guess this fella needs a lesson,' Charlie said, cutting loose with a swinging fist that landed squarely on Drago's jaw, rocking his brain.

Drago staggered back over the saloon hitch rail and fell heavily. Benjy took full advantage of his winded state to wade in and sink a vicious boot in Drago's belly. Bile rushed up his throat. Charlie added another boot to the side of Drago's head which scattered his senses and sent him reeling, but mad as hell.

He glanced Haskin's way, seeing him in tripli-cate as his eyesight seesawed wildly, the way a drunk's might after a week-long bender. From what he could sift from the hazy image of the marshal, Haskin was content to let the odds stack up against him and not intervene. Well, what could he expect? Nate Haskin had made no bones about his intention to steer clear of trouble between him and the Skeltons. A wise choice, judging by the howling approval the Skelton crew's treatment of him was getting. But, Drago reckoned, a man should not wear a badge unless he was prepared to bring honour to it. However, maybe there wasn't that much difference between him and Haskin. He'd worn a badge and had let a killer like Spicer McCall slip the noose waiting for him back in Apache Gulch. The reasons might have been different, but the shame was the same.

Drago was on his knees, trying desperately to get the strength back in his legs to stand up, when he saw Charlie bearing down on him again, his boot coming straight for his face. Anger, coupled with the pride that had been dented by the crowd's jeering laughter at his plight, added up to fury.

Jack Drago grabbed Charlie's boot. He twisted his leg with every smidgen of strength he could muster. The reward for his effort was the pleasurable snap of bone, as Charlie's ankle splintered. Drago shoved the screaming cow-puncher away from him, hard. Charlie spun backwards and landed on the saloon hitch rail, his larynx taking terrible punishment that left him gagging for breath: a breath that was fast running out. His face suffused with a dark, blotched purple. Flecks of spittle and blood formed a foam on his gasping lips, a foam that became more voluminous and red by the second, until blood flowed freely from his mouth, and he stopped breathing.

The shocked interval allowed Drago to regain his strength and composure. When Benjy turned on him in a furious rage, Jack Drago countered his murderous onslaught with a skilful and punishing series of blows that had him reeling back on to the boardwalk. Drago, not of a charitable frame of mind, kept punching until the Skelton man was all but out cold.

Through the thunder of the conflict came the sound of a gun being cocked. Jack Drago spun around, his hand diving for his pistol, and finding to his horror an empty holster. He had lost his gun in the frantic mêlée.

Spicer McCall had him cold!

SEVEN

Through a red haze, Drago saw McCall, his hand hovering over his gun, clawed and ready to draw. But he had not drawn – Nate Haskin's was the gun he had heard being cocked.

'Leave the iron right where it is, McCall,' the marshal ordered. 'If you want to take your chances in a pugilistic contest with Drago, I'll step aside. But I'll not wear a man being gunned down in cold blood.'

McCall's gimlet eyes studied Haskin, trying to gauge his chance against him if he went for iron.

'Don't be a fool,' the lawman cautioned. 'Fisticuffs, or nothing.'

Spicer McCall said with demonic venom: 'You're buying into a mess of trouble, Marshal. Backing this hobo against Sam Skelton.'

'I've no intention of stepping between Skelton and Drago. Their fight is theirs to resolve.'

'I represent Mr Skelton's interest,' McCall told

the lawman. 'You buck me and you buck him, Marshal.'

'I've had enough lip from you, McCall,' Haskin grated. 'Make up your mind. Is this over or not?'

McCall gave a further moment's consideration to his plight, before saying, 'It's over for now.' He strode angrily to his horse and swung into the saddle. 'You stay in town,' he told Benjy. 'Get Charlie boxed. Mr Skelton will want nothing but the best.' He swung the stallion he was astride and pointed the horse towards the south end of town and the Skelton range. He departed at a gallop, but not before he issued a warning to both Jack Drago and Nate Haskin. 'This is not finished by a long shot!'

Under Haskin's scowl, the crowd broke up, most of them drifting back into the saloon in mumbling knots. Drago had no doubt that the topic of conversation was not his spirited comeback, but rather the marshal's wholly unexpected intervention.

'Thanks,' Drago said.

'Damn your thanks, Drago!' Haskin snarled. 'Your presence here has loosed demons who'll be hard to put back in the bottle.' His beefy shoulders slumped wearily. 'In this town we've lost count of the number of strangers who went prodding in Tomb Valley, and never returned.' He considered Drago for a lengthy spell. 'I guess you'd best be thinking about what you want to put on your marker, Drago.'

'That's a mighty shameful admission for a lawman to have to make, Marshal,' Drago said angrily.

For a second the anger in Haskin's eyes matched Jack Drago's. But he quickly shelved his anger, and admitted quietly, 'I guess it is at that, mister.'

The marshal turned and strolled leisurely back to the law office. Drago instantly regretted his criticism, considering his attitude a mighty poor show of thanks for Haskin's timely intervention. He had long ago learned that a man had to deal with life the way he saw fit, and it was not befitting for another man to tell him how he should live that life.

'Do I still have that room?' Drago asked.

'If Alice has little enough sense to have you.'

Drago collected his .45 and pointed his toecaps in the direction of the canary-yellow house at the end of Main. 'Guess there's only one way to find out.'

He was coming to the opening of an alley that ran alongside the Silver Mustang when, in the window of the general store across the street from the alley, he saw the reflection of a man with his back flat against the saloon wall. He recognized a tall, grey-haired man who had joined the crowd outside the saloon, but had not been part of the Silver Mustang crowd who had supported Spicer McCall and the Bent Bough rowdies. He was dressed in town clothes, and had the soft hands of a pen-pusher.

It was only a flash of time between Drago's seeing the man's reflection in the store window, and then the six-gun in his hand. The elderly man, the most unlikely of assassins, sprang from the alley, pistol cocked and raised. He got off a shot, but it was a jittery bullet that whined harmlessly over Drago's head. The thing was, if he had not ducked, the ambusher's bullet would have taken the top of his head clean off.

Briefly, Drago thought about trying to reason with the bushwhacker. However, with the man lining him up in his sights again, he was left with no option but to defend himself. He double triggered his Colt .45, making both bullets count. The first bullet shattered the man's chest, the second his face.

Nate Haskin came running. The crowd piled back out of the saloon. Each face turned Jack Drago's way, hot with anger. He had seen men look like that before, and he recognized lynching fury.

'There was nothing I could do, Marshal,' Drago said. 'It was him or me. And seeing that he made the running, I don't understand why I'm the butt

84

end of your and the town's anger.'

Haskin bent over the soft-skinned man to check for a pulse.

'Someone get the doc,' Drago said, in the hope that his bullets had not fatally wounded the man, but he held out little hope of that being the case.

No one moved. Haskin gave the reason why.

'You just killed him, Drago. You've just shot Doc Crowe.'

Jack Drago was stunned. 'Why would the doc...?'

'Simple,' Haskin explained. 'Like most folk in this town, Doc was beholden to Sam Skelton. Doc Crowe had a fondness for liquor and cards, a bad combination for any man to be ensnared by. Got into all sorts of trouble, and was pretty much washed up until Sam Skelton stepped in to clear his debts and pay for treatment in a fancy 'Frisco clinic.'

The lawman sighed, heavy shouldered.

'I guess Doc reckoned that he might do Skelton a favour. You weren't the kind to be scared off as easily as the others who tried to put down roots on Skelton range.'

Angered by Haskin's remarks, and saddened by the death of a foolish old man, Drago exploded. 'It isn't all Skelton range. The north end of the valley is free range, for any man to stake his claim to. When is this town going to get that fact through its head!'

The grim-faced crowd pressed forward. Haskin filled the gap. He announced: 'I'm arresting you for the murder of Doc Crowe, Drago.'

This statement got a fiery rebuff.

'Just hang him, Haskin,' a man from the crowd hollered, and got near unanimous support.

'It wasn't murder,' Drago argued, and accused Haskin. 'You must have seen what happened? You were on your way back to the marshal's office.'

'The facts will be presented to a court of law,' Haskin said. 'A jury will then decide.'

Drago backed off Haskin, ready to make a stand. He'd be damned if he was going tamely to a certain noose.

Tiredly, Nate Haskin said: 'There must be a hundred guns in that crowd, Drago. All pointed your way.' He paused. 'But I reckon the one that's most deadly is held by Doc Crowe's widow, standing right behind you.'

Jack Drago felt the prod of a rifle in his spine, and heard the crying of the woman he'd made a widow.

EIGHT

The tremor of anger in the woman's hand sent shivers along Jack Drago's spine. He reckoned that she was only a second away from blasting him into eternity.

'Easy now, Mamie,' the marshal counselled. 'Let the law deal with this.'

'Law?' she spat out tearfully. 'What law, Nate Haskin? You bowed out a long time ago.'

Haskin's face screwed up, as if slapped hard.

'This is not the time to discuss the ins and outs of the past, Mamie,' he said. 'Put down the rifle. Drago's headed for jail.'

'And he'll hang, too,' Judge Wes Lane pronounced to the baying crowd.

Haskin scowled at the judge's intervention. It served no useful purpose. All it did was whip up an already excited crowd. And it also made it obvious that any trial over which Wes Lane presided would be swift, tainted, and downright prejudicial to Jack Drago. But a fair trial in Abbot Creek, in which Sam Skelton had an interest, was something that had not happened for a long time. Wes Lane called himself a judge, but the only knowledge of the law he had, had been acquired from pamphlets and leaflets which he had picked up here and there, and had welded into a version of the law that bore no relationship at all to the real article. He had arrived in Abbot Creek three years previously, dispensing legal argument from the back of a wagon that bore the sign:

JUDGE WESLEY LANE, ATTORNEY-AT-LAW.

He had been successful in the representations he had made on behalf of the hardcases he had represented, simply because he could deliver a rousing spiel, and there was no one around Abbot Creek who could contradict the fancy words he strung together. Wes Lane's greatest asset was that he mouthed off like a lawyer. In the West, sounding right was often more important than actually being right.

'Nothing like a fair trial to give a man hope, Marshal,' Jack Drago said.

Nate Haskin figured that he had no option but to arrest Drago. If he had not, he'd have been lynched or gunned down for sure – Doc Crowe had been a very popular man in Abbot Creek. Drago could not watch his back all the time. Abbot Creek was full of men ready to ingratiate themselves with Sam Skelton. And there were many men who owed Skelton, and would hope that if they bagged Drago, he would quash their indebtedness to him. And there were those, like the town no-goods, who would kill Jack Drago just because they had been handed an excuse to indulge their mean natures.

By shackling Jack Drago unjustly, Haskin had handed himself a thorny problem. As Drago had rightly accused, he had indeed witnessed what had happened and knew Jack Drago's innocence. He could press ahead with a rigged trial which, in essence, would simply make Drago's lynching official, and sink him lower in the mire into which he had stepped the first time he had turned a blind eye to Sam Skelton's skulduggery.

Or he could make a stand.

It was a dilemma he could have done without. His fears for Alice, pretty much in abeyance since he'd become blind to Sam Skelton's wrongdoing, now rushed back to haunt him. It was that fear which had made him turn away from the man whom Skelton had been bull-whipping outside the saloon, in what seemed an age ago now.

Alice was a gentle, kind woman, ill-equipped to face the rigours of widowhood. Sam Skelton had made it plain on a visit to the law office that day, before he had hauled the man out of the Silver Mustang, that, should he intervene in the man's punishment, Alice would face such a future. Haskin had told himself that there was little he could have done with the odds stacked against him – Skelton had ridden in backed by ten men. But it was no consolation. He wore a badge, and had taken an oath. Both of which he had dishonoured on that infamous day.

Now, not a night went by without the stranger's screams haunting his dreams, the same screams he had listened to secreted away in his office that day, screams that had become an agonized whimper by the time Rick Skelton had finished with him.

He had skulked that day. And had been skulking since.

'We'll have the trial ...' Wes Lane, cutting in on Haskin's reverie, consulted his pocket watch, 'at four o'clock sharp, Marshal.'

'That's only an hour from now,' Haskin said, shocked.

'Plenty of time to swear in a jury,' Lane said. 'In fact why wait an hour? Haul him into the saloon right now. Five minutes is all it should take to form a jury. Any volunteers?'

There was no shortage. Willing volunteers crowded around Lane.

'See, Marshal,' Lane scoffed. 'No problem in getting a jury together.'

Haskin, in a quandary, came up with a lie.

'I need to visit home first, Judge. Alice has been feeling poorly. I want to check on her.'

'This will take no time at all,' Lane flung back.

His uncaring stance caused a ripple of unease among the majority of the crowd. Haskin had long ago lost the respect of most men in town, but Alice Haskin was looked on with fondness.

Fred Eager, the hardware-store owner, spoke up.

'I reckon an hour will be just fine, Judge. It'll give the marshal time to see to his wife, and it will give the stranger a chance to make his peace with his Maker.'

Lane was of a mind to buck Eager, but instead showed an oily smile. 'If you say so, Fred. Then it's fine by me.'

Eager was the chairman of the town council. An upright man, who for a time had tried to get Sam Skelton to moderate his stance, but, like the marshal, had bowed, fearing as Nate Haskin did for the safety of those he cared for. He did not like Wes Lane, picking him out early on as nothing more than a shyster with a glib tongue. His dislike of Lane had steadily deepened when he became Sam Skelton's pawn, ready to do his bidding without qualm.

Wes Lane feared Eager. He had tried a couple of times to dislodge him from the town council, and had almost succeeded. Lane knew that if he were to lose his seat on the council, his standing in the town, and his ability to smooth Sam Skelton's path would be greatly diminished. Sooner or later, he was betting on out-smarting Eager, and seeing the back of him. Until then he was prepared to be patient and bide his time. His long-term plan was to ride on Sam Skelton's coat-tails all the way to political office. Washington was Wes Lane's intended final stop, right along-side Sam Skelton.

Lane was Sam Skelton's lackey, owing his lofty position to the rancher's patronage. It was Skelton who had him appointed a judge, and he'd continue to use his office to remove any thorns in Skelton's side, thorns like Jack Drago.

''Preciate your concern, Fred,' Haskin thanked Eager.

'An hour, Marshal,' Lane reminded Haskin. 'Not a minute longer.' He turned to two toerags stand-ing near him, who were never far away from his side. 'Spike – Bart, you boys stand guard over the prisoner while the marshal is tending to his domestic chores.'

Wes Lane settled snake eyes on Drago.

'If he blinks, feel free to dispense with a trial.'

Spike, a lanky string of a man, with a jagged scar running the length of his right cheek, no doubt inflicted by a broken bottle in a saloon brawl, swaggered forward.

'You got it, Judge.'

Nate Haskin stepped in front of Spike to block his path to Drago.

'I won't be needing you fellas for a spell.'

Spike glanced back to Lane for instructions.

'Paperwork needs doing,' the marshal explained.

Lane laughed. 'Sure, Marshal. We wouldn't want anyone to say that we hanged a man without the right paperwork.'

Lane's remarks got a guffaw from the crowd trailing the judge into the saloon.

'Are you a praying man, Drago?' Haskin asked.

'Just let's say that I'm not that well known in heaven, Marshal.'

'Well,' the lawman sighed, 'if you've got ground to make up, then you'd better start now.'

As they walked to the jail, Drago asked: 'Are you going to just let them drag me out and string me up?'

The lawman stopped and looked hard into Drago's eyes.

'Let's get one thing straight, Drago,' he chewed. 'This mess is of your own making. Therefore,' he concluded brusquely, 'the price you pay is of your own making, too.'

'Aren't you forgetting one small point, Marshal,' Drago said waspishly. 'Whatever foolishness there is on my part, I'm not a murderer.'

Haskin closed his eyes, and his shoulders

slumped in resignation.

'In this town, fella,' he told Drago. 'You're whatever Sam Skelton says you are. That's the point I've been trying to get through that rock head of yours since you dropped by my office.'

His resignation sharpened.

'And the next lesson for learning is, that no one hereabouts can do a damn thing about that, Drago.'

NINE

Nate Haskin slammed the cell door shut on Drago, just as Alice Haskin put in an appearance.

'What in tarnation are you doing out on the street, Alice?' he fretted. 'It ain't safe.'

The marshal's wife stepped aside of her husband to study Drago with a long, lingering look.

'Doesn't look like a killer to me,' she said, her small mouth fixed in a determined pout. 'You've got to cut him loose, Nate.'

'Cut him loose?' Haskin yelped. 'Don't talk loco, woman.'

'You cut him loose, or you're not sharing my bed or eating at my table again,' she threatened.

Haskin, not taking kindly to being scolded in front of another man, snarled, 'You look after the house, Alice. And I'll look after the law.'

'Well,' Alice Haskin chirped, 'if I looked after the house the way you look after the law – hah!

Then we'd sure have a nice how-do-you-do.'

The marshal scowled on seeing Jack Drago's wry smile.

'You won't be smiling when they'll hang you,' he spat.

'There'll be no hanging,' Alice said.

'Oh,' Haskin glowered. 'And why the hell not, woman?'

'Don't you swear in my presence, Nate Haskin,' she rebuked him. 'Keep that kind of talk for your cronies in the saloon.' Alice's jaw set in a grim line. 'And there'll be no hanging, because I saw what happened, and it's a clear-cut case of self-defence. Doc Crowe tried to bushwhack your prisoner. Left him with no choice but to shoot back.'

She came face to face with her husband.

'And that's what I'll be saying in court, Marshal Haskin.'

'Stay out of this, Alice,' Haskin pleaded.

'Can't. I won't see a man strung up on the wrong.'

'There's hope for the town yet,' Drago observed drily.

'Mind your own damn business, Drago,' the lawman bellowed.

'It's my neck,' Drago flung back. 'That makes it my business.'

'Well, what're you waiting for?' Alice said. 'Turn Mr Drago loose, Nate.'

'I guess we're just about in time, Bart,' Spike,

one of the men appointed by Wes Lane to oversee Drago's incarceration during Haskin's absence said, standing in the open law-office door.

'Sure looks that way,' Bart growled.

Spike strolled into the office. 'You made a good recovery ma'am,' he said to Alice.

'Recovery?'

'Never you mind, Alice,' Haskin said.

'From that illness that Nate was rushing home to check on you for, ma'am,' Spike said.

'I ain't been a day sick since I was sixteen years old,' Alice feistily pronounced.

'Then,' Bart sniggered, 'you sure've been healthy for a long time, ma'am.'

Nate Haskin's fist shot out and catapulted Bart back against the door. Spitting fire, Wes Lane's lapdog's hand dropped to his gun. The marshal, anticipating Bart's reaction, followed through and laid the barrel of his pistol on the crown of his head. Bart slumped to his knees, moaning.

'No need for that, Marshal,' Spike growled. 'Bart was only leg-pullin'.'

'Get out and take that cur with you,' Haskin ordered Spike.

Cockily, Spike said: 'Well, you see, I figure you've got to get the judge's say-so to be mouthin' orders like that, Marshal. 'Seein' that me and Bart were 'pointed by the judge to act as his agents.' His snake-mean eyes flashed to Alice and

97

back to Haskin. 'Now, I wonder why you lied 'bout your missus being poorly, Marshal? Mebbe the judge would think that you were plannin' on pervertin' the course of justice?'

Alice Haskin scoffed. 'What justice? Mr Drago acted in self-defence and has been unjustly caboosed.'

Spike snorted. 'You sayin' that the marshal is crooked, ma'am?'

Alice Haskin looked at her husband and stated uncompromisingly: 'If he lets this man stand trial in front of a Lane-rigged jury … Yes. That's what I'm saying, mister.'

Drago could see that Nate Haskin wanted to crawl into the mouse-hole in the skirting behind his desk. Alice took his hands in hers, her eyes glowing with love.

'Nate, honey. This is your chance to wear that badge with pride again. The way you used to, when you first pinned it on.'

'You let that murderer walk off free,' Spike warned, 'and Sam Skelton will have your badge, Marshal. And then your hide, too.'

'Don't you worry none about me,' Alice told the dithering marshal. 'You do what you have to, Nate. What you should have done a long time ago.'

Haskin took his wife in his arms and hugged her. 'You're a darn fine woman, Alice. The best a man could have around.'

'You goin' to let Drago walk?' Wes Lane's agent snarled.

'Can't rightly hold him,' Haskin said, turning to open the cell door. 'Alice saw it happen. Says that it was a clear-cut case of self-defence.'

'Kinda convenient, ain't it?' Spike grumbled.

Haskin paused in opening the cell door. When he turned to face Lane's man, his eyes glowed with a vibrant anger.

'Are you calling Alice a liar?' he asked hotly.

The stand-off lasted a full minute, before Spike shrugged. 'Sorry Mrs Haskin, ma'am. Didn't mean no offence.'

Alice's riposte was thornily scornful.

'To be offended I'd have to think something of you, Spike Haines. I don't!'

The marshal turned back to open the cell door. Drago grabbed his six-gun from its holster.

'What the dev...?' the lawman yelped.

Drago triggered the six-gun, just as Haines sneaked his pistol from its holster. The bullet smashed his shoulder, and left slivers of glistening, ragged bone showing through. Spike Haines collapsed back against the door and slid to the floor, howling like a wounded animal.

'He'd have backshot you,' Drago told Haskin.

'Should've seen it coming.' Nate Haskin's weariness was a thousand years old. 'I guess I'm getting too long in the tooth to be toting a badge.'

The sound of gunfire curtailed the rowdiness in the charged atmosphere of the Silver Mustang saloon, where twelve chairs were lined up left of the stage for the jury which had been sworn in by Wes Lane, each and every man hand-picked to deliver the verdict that would remove Drago as a thorn from Sam Skelton's side.

Lane led the charge to the jail.

'Just a minute, Judge,' said one of the jury members, a scruffy-looking no-account man who scrounged free drinks from whoever was willing to provide them, and who might need his fists, boots, knife or gun to render a service. 'Don't know who's at the other side of that door. Spike or Bart ain't showed.'

Wes Lane stopped dead in his tracks.

'Good thinking, Frank,' Lane complimented the free-drinks chaser, blanching at his intemperate eagerness to be of service to Sam Skelton. No dead man ever made it to Washington, he reminded himself.

Frank hammered with the butt of his six-gun on the law-office door. 'Spike...? Bart? What's happenin' in there?'

The Lane hangers-on crowding round the door scattered when Nate Haskin yanked it open, pistol cocked, Jack Drago standing alongside him in like fashion. Wes Lane was first to find his voice.

'Are you breaking your own prisoner out of jail, Marshal Haskin?'

'Drago's no longer a prisoner, Lane.'

'That'll be Judge Lane, sir,' he growled. He waved his hand in a sweeping arc. 'I believe that that decision is for these good citizens to make, Haskin.'

'Not if Drago didn't do anything wrong,' the marshal answered.

Lane scoffed. 'I'd say shooting the town doctor was doing wrong.'

Spike put in an appearance, nursing his shattered shoulder. 'Marshal's missus says she saw what happened. Says that Drago acted in self-defence, Judge.'

Alice Haskin stepped forward. 'That's the way it was, Lane.'

Again, Wes Lane reacted angrily.

'Like I said. That'll be Judge Lane, ma'am,' he said sourly.

'Fiddly,' Alice Haskin flung back. 'A dumb-headed mule knows as much about the law as you ever did, Wes Lane.'

Lane's face became mottled with anger.

'You have no call to—'

'Oh, go shove your head in a bucket,' Alice interjected. 'You're nothing but a stuffed-shirt windbag, in the pay of Sam Skelton.'

The atmosphere electrified. Wes Lane, Haskin

knew, was a dangerous man. It took a lot to push him to his limit, because he was counting on riding Sam Skelton's coat-tails to Washington, so he needed a veneer of respectability. But Alice's tirade might just have pushed him to that limit, beyond which he could turn as mean as a cornered rat. There were men behind him who, on his say-so, would not hesitate to silence any of his opponents. Haskin knew, to his discredit, that it would not be the first time that Wes Lane had had opposition to him removed. He could never prove as much, because Lane was a canny sort, who never took a hand in the actions he orchestrated. However, Nate Haskin knew that he should have run the shyster judge out of Abbot Creek a long time ago. Long before Sam Skelton had cottoned on to Lane's use in protecting and promoting his agenda.

Wes Lane's spite almost overcame his good sense, but at the last second he got his anger under control and scoffingly dismissed Alice Haskin's accusations.

'I've got a string of law degrees on my office walls, Alice,' he said silkily. 'You're free to visit and inspect them any time of your choosing.'

Alice was equally scoffing in her retort. 'Dime store wall-dressing, Lane.'

'That's mighty loose talk, Alice,' Lane said smoothly. There was a smile on his lips, but a threat in his eyes. 'A man's got a right to protect his reputation from such a spiteful tongue.'

Lane had never been confronted with such forthright ferocity, and feared the effect Alice Haskin's challenge would have, both on the immediate crowd and the town in general when word of it spread.

In that second, Jack Drago could understand all of Nate Haskin's fears for his wife. He had no doubt at all that, pushed far enough, Wes Lane would not hesitate to take whatever action was necessary to keep a tight rein on the plans he had worked out for himself.

Drago reckoned that in his panic Lane was a whisper away from silencing Alice Haskin. Even in his limited view of the crowd milling around the law-office door, with the exception of Lane's own rowdies, Alice's words had started folk thinking.

Alice had the same recognition and fearlessly pressed home the advantage she had won.

'The good folk of this town should run you out, Lane. And make this the kind of town we were once proud of. A good town, with decent people.'

Alice shunted aside her husband's attempt to sideline her.

'A town with principles and justice. Where an honest man's rights, such as Mr Drago's, are respected, and his claim to free range upheld.'

A tall, rangy man said: 'I'd sure like a piece of Tomb Valley m'self, Alice.'

'It's your right, John,' she replied. 'It's every man's right, as long as there's free range to meet those rights.'

'Everyone knows that Tomb Valley is Sam Skelton's domain,' Lane said. Addressing the swiftly swelling crowd, he continued: 'It makes no sense to me to have a whole lot of small farms and ranches cluttering up the valley, when the Bent Bough can bring prosperity beyond your dreams to the town.'

This was an opinion championed by the judge's backers.

Lane went on: 'The fact is, that the bigger the Bent Bough gets, the more prosperous this town will become.'

Wes Lane's speech got another rousing round of approval from his and Skelton's cronies.

But the man whom Alice Haskin had addressed as John held fast to his view, and backed Alice's assertion that while there was free range for the claiming, every man had the right to it.

'Mebbe it's time this town stood up to Sam Skelton,' he chanted.

Wes Lane paled on hearing the ringing endorsement that reached all the way back to the saloon from where the crowd started. There was opposition, too, of course, for one reason or another. There was no small measure of fear of Sam Skelton's wrath, which could make a man penniless at least, and dead at worst.

Wes Lane, to his utter horror, witnessed the seeds of rebellion budding. Determined not to be robbed of the prize he had set his cap at, a lap-of-luxury life in Washington, he decided there and then that the embryonic rebellion would have to be crushed.

He'd make plans accordingly, and quickly.

Seeing the dread that haunted Nate Haskin's face as he protectively drew Alice into his arms, Jack Drago began to regret that he had not heeded the lawman's advice and ridden on. His stubborn ambition to settle in Tomb Valley had stirred a hornets' nest that would not settle down again until one side of the coming feud surrendered or was wiped out.

Maybe there was still time to head out...?

TEN

Beth Crofton tossed restlessly in her sleep, the guilt of her dreams making her uneasy. Because the man she was sharing those dreams with was Jack Drago. She came awake, breaking the encirclement of Drago's arms, her body never before as alive to carnal sensation as it was at that moment. Since he had held her in his arms, the fiery, sinful feelings he had stirred in her had persisted unceasingly.

The moment she had seen Drago ride across the valley to Brown's Creek, her heart had done a crazy jig. She had been in the shady dell overlooking the creek, not by design, ready to intervene if Rick Skelton's anger reached the killing pitch it often did, but because she wanted to secretly view this stranger who had set her heart skittering, like no man ever had. Her mood since had been one of high hope and deepest despair. She had no right to feel the way she did, when she was owned by another man. Because in the West, that's what a woman was – owned. As much a man's property as the horses in the corral or the plough in the barn. She was Ben Crofton's wife and therefore his property. If she were to forsake him, irrespective of his often callous and demeaning ways, she would find no sympathy or comfort, even from the women who shared her suffering. In the West the old adage of making your bed and lying on it was never more true.

Beth got out of bed and put a woollen shawl over her shoulders. The cabin, which Crofton grandiosely called a ranch house, consisted of only two rooms. It was bitterly cold, with more snow falling, and Beth would welcome the heat of the fire in the other room, by which her husband was sprawled in his drunken stupor. But, rather than disturb him and suffer another tirade of rot-gut abuse, Beth sat by the bedroom window dreaming her dreams, as she had so often done in the nights after her mother had died and her father entertained his women, introducing Rick to their delights, too. Her dreams now – as then – were dreams of freedom. Then she wanted nothing more than to escape from the Bent Bough. Now, she wanted nothing more than to nestle in Jack Drago's arms. Was she, Beth thought, destined continuously to dream and never find happiness?

Sitting perfectly still, looking out at the wind-tossed snow, Beth Crofton's thoughts returned to Jack Drago. She dreamed the dreams of a girl, but felt the fiery desires of a woman.

It had been a long time since Drago had slept in such a soft bed, and it was taking a hell of a time to adjust to lying on something that had no rocks under it. At least that's what he told himself to explain away his wakefulness, when his body was bone tired.

Beth Crofton was the real reason, and a reason he did not want to think about. His troubles were many and piling higher all the time, without drawing the wrath of an angry husband on his head, and adding fuel to the fire between him and Sam Skelton.

Beth Crofton is just another woman, he kept telling himself. A woman's a woman, was another phrase which kept popping up in his mind. But he knew that he was lying to himself. Beth was not *just* another woman. She was the missing piece in a lifetime of searching.

Judge Wes Lane was not in bed. He had visitors. Two cut-throats in his employ who had as much conscience as Satan has good intentions. But even they were uneasy with the task Lane needed them to do.

'Burn down the marshal's house?' a runtish

man by the name of Curly Yokam, shifting uneasily in his chair, questioned the judge.

'Why would ya wanna to do that, Judge?' the second man asked. A stringy specimen with a right eye that jumped all over the place, due to a damaged facial nerve that had been severed in a knife fight in a cantina in Nogales. 'Curly and me can just ambush this fella Drago. Right, Curly?'

'Sure thing, Judge,' Yokam said. 'Me and Danny's real good at creepin' up on a man.'

Lane cursed silently that it was his misfortune to be surrounded by half-wits. He explained. 'Drago is only part of the problem. Alice Haskin's mouth could stir a whole mess of trouble, like it did outside the jail. That kind of independence I can do without – so can Sam Skelton. Why, Alice Haskin almost had a bevy of claim-stakers heading for Tomb Valley.'

'Yeah, Alice is a feisty one, sure 'nuff,' Yokam said, with no small amount of admiration.

'I hear she got her old man's engine firing today, too,' Danny added.

'You work for me,' Lane snarled. 'You go and draw your pay elsewhere if you want to start an Alice Haskin admiration society, you hear?'

Suitably chastised, the two men settled down to listen to Wes Lane's reasons for burning down Nate and Alice Haskin's home.

'Haskin, fired up the way he's been by Alice, has

taken an unhealthy turn towards honesty. With Drago to back him, that could mean big trouble.' He poured two generous whiskeys for his visitors, the kind of whiskey that slides mellowly down the gullet. 'A bullet in the back, in the town's present mood, might not go unquestioned. But a fire ...' He sneered. 'Well, fires are accidents, aren't they? They happen all the time.' He replenished their glasses, chuckling. 'But the end result of an accident can be the very same as a bushwhacking, which you fellas never drew the line at.'

'Never killed no woman though,' Yokam said, uneasy with the idea.

Lane sneered. 'I'm sure when I tell you that you'll get an extra hundred dollars, your conscience won't be so keen, Curly.'

'A hundred,' the man called Danny yelped, his dodgy eye wildly rolling.

'A hundred dollars to men who scraped by was a temptation that overrode all their qualms. They were already grabbing the tins of kerosene which Lane kept in store to fuel the many lamps he had around the expensive house, purchased with the proceeds from his myriad underhanded dealings. He checked his gold pocket-watch.

'Fifteen after midnight. I reckon everyone should be asleep by now, gents.'

'Pa...? You in there?' Sam Skelton came out of his

reverie as Rick Skelton burst through the sitting-room door. 'Something wrong, Pa? Ain't like you to be unable to sleep.'

Skelton senior looked away from the leaping flames of the log fire, and for the first time, as if his eyes had just opened after a long blindness, he saw his bastard son for what he was, a snivelling cur. The offspring of an unholy union.

'Wha'cha looking at her picture for?' Rick snarled, pointing to the picture of Ellie Skelton which Sam was reverently and lovingly gazing at, his eyes awash with memories.

'Guess as a man gets older he dreams more,' Sam Skelton said. 'And I've been dreaming a lot lately, Rick.'

' 'Bout what? That bitch?'

Sam Skelton's hand shot out and slapped Rick Skelton's face, hard. 'Don't talk about Ellie that way ever again!'

Rick Skelton massaged his stinging cheek. 'I'm your son,' he defiantly flung back. 'I mostly run this ranch, now that you've more or less lost the will to.' He grabbed another photograph off the piano; the picture of the saloon whore who bore him. He thrust it at Sam Skelton. 'She's my ma, rest her soul,' he fumed. 'And the rightful woman in this house.'

Sam Skelton held his son's stare. 'I'm going to ask Beth to come home, Rick.'

'Beth?' Rick snorted, his anger reaching rage. 'And I suppose she'll be bringing 'long that no-good Crofton, too?'

'Ben Crofton is Beth's husband. Not the man Beth would have chosen, if I hadn't my heart shut to caring, and my eyes closed to reason.'

'I got the right to my say, Pa,' Rick argued.

'You have your say, Rick.' Sam Skelton sprang out of his chair. 'But I'm not going to change my mind.' He strode to the door and swung about before leaving the room to rock Rick Skelton back on his heels. 'Another thing, I've decided to let Drago stay in the valley.'

'You what?' Rick yelped. 'Have you taken leave of your senses?'

'There's been too much killing, and too much bitterness,' Sam Skelton said wearily. 'I should have realized a long time ago that this valley is big enough for whoever wants to farm or ranch it.'

'Are you forgetting all those extra cows needing grass come spring?'

'I haven't forgotten. We'll buy feed from the likes of Drago. He'll need the cash, so he'll be happy to sell. Then,' he said with finality, 'the Bent Bough will put down firm boundaries and trim the herd to suit Skelton range.'

'You've gone loco,' Rick growled menacingly.

'No,' Sam said. 'But,' he looked at the photograph of Ellie Skelton which he still held, 'I've been loco for a long time. Now, I'm sane. Tomorrow I'll ride into town and tell Drago that he can stake his claim, along with any other man wanting to. Then I'll swing by Beth's place and ask her to come home to the Bent Bough, where she belongs.'

When Sam left the room, Rick Skelton dropped weakly into a chair, his thoughts in turmoil. The Bent Bough was about to be grabbed from his grasp. He was certain that the queer turn of mind which Sam had had, would hand the ranch to Beth and that no-good husband of hers by default.

Slowly, he marshalled his spinning brain, and began to plan in the devious way he could. As his plan took shape, he was sure that he was on the right track. No one was going to take the Bent Bough away from him.

No one.

Not even Sam Skelton.

ELEVEN

The men on Wes Lane's dirty-deed errand hopped from shadow to shadow as they made their way along Main to Haskin's house. They could have taken a route through the town's backlots, which would have been their preferred choice, but the judge had pointed out the dangers of stumbling over one of the many hobos who used the various shacks, many of them the remnants of the one-room homes the first settlers in Abbot Creek had built, while others were the abandoned hopes of more ambitious men, whose dream of riches had vanished when they found themselves on the wrong end of Sam Skelton's ire.

The ghostly hulks could, at any second, yield up any down-and-outs who might just remember Curly Yokam and his sidekick's passage. It would not be difficult to link them to Lane, not that anyone would likely want to, with the marshal, his wife, and Drago burned to cinders. But Wes

114

Lane, being a man who had reached his present lofty prominence by not taking risks, was not about to take one now. A careful and planning man, he liked, as far as was possible, to reduce the odds in his favour, which he had been successfully doing for a long time.

Of course, the more direct route along Main had its possible pitfalls too. But not as many as the backlots might spring. Seeing a man making his way along Main, even in the cautious manner Curly Yokam and Danny were proceeding, was less hazardous and more explainable, should an explanation be needed, than skulking through the town's seamy side.

Questions, once the Haskins' house burned down, was what Wes Lane wanted to avoid like the plague.

As Wes Lane's merchants of mayhem made their careful way towards the canary-yellow house, their scrutiny of Abbot Creek's main drag was concentrated on reaching the house unseen. Had they glanced behind them, they might have seen the judge dodging into the doors they had just vacated. But likely not, too. Because Wes Lane had the ability, learned over a long and devious career in skulduggery, to sink into shadows with the ease of a ghost.

Ten miles east of Abbot Creek, there was another

man hugging shadows. Rick Skelton had lain awake, biding his time until the household settled down. As he crept from his bedroom, boots in hand, the hall clock struck two, its chimes jangling his already raw nerves. He paused in his stockinged feet to listen to the sounds of the house, anxious to pick up the slightest hint of discovery. Satisfied that he was prowling alone, he quickly but quietly made his way downstairs to Sam Skelton's den. Entering, he carefully eased the door shut. Feeling safer now, he dispensed with some of his caution. He made his way to Sam's desk, where he took a sheet of notepaper and pen from the desk drawer. He tried to write by the light of the moon, but its light was too fitful yet with the breaking snowclouds flitting across its face. He would have to risk lighting the desk lamp, which he hadn't wanted to do. The last thing he wanted was to be discovered prowling about in the still of night, with the questions that would bring.

He lit the lamp, keeping the flame at its lowest. He shaded the lamp's glow with his hat, directing the light directly down on the note he was writing. Of course, it could still be seen by a keen-eyed ranch hand paying a visit to the privy near the bunkhouse. Unlikely on such a bitter night. But it was on such chance that a man's luck sometimes turned sour.

Not a man used to stringing words together, Rick Skelton's task in composing the note to Jack Drago was a laboured one. He wisely kept it simple. It read:

Dear Jack,
Meet me at Crazy Gap at eight thirty. Take the
trail east from town for four miles. This is our
secret.
    Beth.

It was a clever ruse, taking advantage of the spark between Beth and Jack Drago. Rick was counting on a clandestine meeting with Beth proving irresistible to Drago. Rick Skelton quenched the lamp. He went to the den window to look out on the snowy landscape, his eyes searching for any movement. He saw no one, and there were no footprints in the pristine snow.

He was safe.

His next danger would come when he went to the stables to collect his horse. He had cleverly, in so far as he could, dressed in light-coloured clothes, to help him blend in with the snowy whiteness.

He left the house through the kitchen door and, carrying a broom, he made careful and watchful progress across the yard, using the broom to erase any sign of his passage. The snow had stopped and the moon was out, so he could not take a chance on further snow to cover his tracks. Ten minutes later, saddled up, he walked his horse a distance from the house, again using the broom to eliminate signs of his passage. He did not mount up until he was well clear of the house. Once in the saddle, he made tracks for Abbot Creek to deliver his faked note to Jack Drago, as fast as the treacherous conditions would allow.

A ranch hand, returning earlier from town, had mentioned that Nate Haskin had given Drago lodgings. As information, it was gold. The last thing he needed was to have to hawk around Abbot Creek seeking out Jack Drago's doss.

In the snowy night, huddled low in the saddle against the bitter wind, Rick Skelton should have had no cause to be as happy and contented as he was. However, he had every reason to be. The plan he had set in motion would hand him the Bent Bough; lock, stock, and barrel.

'Damn,' Jack Drago swore, rolling around restlessly in the comfortable feather bed.

Thoughts of Beth Crofton would not let him rest; thoughts which he had no right to, Beth being another man's woman. He'd make one more adjustment, and if that didn't work he'd brew a cup of coffee and read a book from Nate Haskin's surprisingly well-stocked library. The marshal called them his porch rocker books.

'I plan to read every one when I hand in my badge,' he'd told Drago over supper.

'Which should have been before now,' Alice had scolded him.

When her husband had stepped outside to the porch to smoke a quirley after supper, Alice Haskin had confided her worries to Drago about the threat to the lawman.

'Now that I've wrenched him free of his blindness, Mr Drago,' she'd said. Then, becoming reflective, 'But I guess maybe it's worth the risk. Just to see Nate stand tall and proud again.'

'Nate was only backing off trouble because he was worried that a ruffled Sam Skelton might be a threat to your well-being, Alice,' Drago confided in return.

'My well-being?' Alice was bemused.

Drago said: 'Nate's fear was that you'd be left alone – a widow.'

Alice's bemusement increased. 'Sam Skelton would never harm me.'

'Do I detect a note of approval for Sam Skelton, Alice?' Drago asked puzzled.

'Almost married Sam once.'

'Married?' Drago chuckled. 'Why, ma'am, you sure are a bundle of surprises.'

'Oh, Sam went right off the rails, true enough. But he's not the first man to have gone wild. And he won't be the last neither.' Alice had leaned closer. 'Tell you, Mr Drago. Wes Lane. Now there's a viper who needs watching. And Rick Skelton,' Alice Haskin's face became gallish, 'he's bad through and through. It does Sam no credit at all, and I've told him so more than once, that he allows that no-good son of his to lead him by the nose into trouble.'

'Sam Skelton,' Drago said, 'doesn't come across as a man who could be led in any direction but the one he wanted to travel in, Alice.'

Alice Haskin's soft eyes reflected the lamplight, as her mind drifted back in time to the long trek West which had taken more than a year to complete due to a mountain of obstacles, before most of the pioneers, exhausted, finally put down roots in Abbot Creek. A couple of months before the wagon train had started out, Sam Skelton had made his proposal of marriage. But already Alice Brennan's eyes were for Nate Haskin only.

'Sometimes I blame myself for Sam's contrary doings,' she sighed. 'He took my refusal badly. A week later, he married Ellie King. Ellie was second best, and she knew it. But Sam and she would have settled, if Ellie could have had more children ...'

She shook her head sadly.

'Beth Skelton is a fine woman, too. Has all of her mother's caring qualities.'

Jack Drago would not offer any argument against that.

'And Sam Skelton should have accepted her as the Lord's blessing! Sam had no call to have that snivelling cur, Rick, with a saloon woman.

'I told him fair and square that if he'd married me, he wouldn't even have had Beth. But he'd laugh, and curse sometimes, too, and say that if he had bedded me he'd have a whole posse of fine sons.' She said sternly: 'I told him shush his mouth. That I figured the fault was in me, and not Nate.'

Just then Haskin strolled back in from the porch, and Alice changed to talking about the weather and a stack of other unimportant things.

'Guess it's turning-in time, Alice,' Nate said, and went on ahead.

Before she left the sitting-room, Alice grabbed Jack Drago's hands and implored; 'If Nate needs help, will you stand with him?'

Drago pondered her request. Backing Nate Haskin had not come into his figuring now that he'd decided to quit Abbot Creek and Tomb Valley.

Fearfully, Alice said: 'Once backbone is lost, it sometimes deserts a man again, and just when he thinks he's found it.'

'The truth is, Alice, that I planned on riding on tomorrow.'

'Riding on?' she asked, astonished. Then she

shook her head in open wonder. 'Why, Jack Drago, you could knock me down with a feather.' Her voice held a note of crushing disappointment. 'Because I hadn't figured you for a man who'd be pushed. Even by Sam Skelton.'

She went off to bed, shoulders slumped. It was then that Drago saw the photograph of Art Leary with his arm looped around Nate Haskin's shoulder, both men grinning like fellas who'd found El Dorado.

'Alice ...' She turned wearily, but her weariness vanished like smoke from a bottle when Drago said, 'If Nate asks, I'll back him. But I won't crowd him.'

'Fair enough. What made you change your mind?'

'A ghost.'

'Huh?'

Drago smiled. 'A long story, Alice. Needs time for telling.'

' 'Night, Jack.'

' 'Night, Alice.'

Wes Lane watched from the shadows as Curly Yokam and his sidekick Danny set about their task, pouring kerosene on the walls of the marshal's timber-frame house. The wood would be surface-wet from the first snowfall, but should quickly catch fire after the long, dry spring and summer which had preceded a cold but dry Fall. And the liberal coating of yellow paint should make the house a raging inferno in no time at all.

Lane watched excitedly as Yokam and Danny circled the house, following his instructions to the letter. The stench of kerosene took the snowy freshness from the night air. He'd wait until the house was well alight before shooting the men and raising the alarm. If he worked it right, Lane reckoned, he could turn out to be the hero of the hour. He'd make sure to be seen charging the house, but, of course, losing out to the flames. That, on top of nailing the duo who had started the blaze, should raise his standing no end.

TWELVE

Rick Skelton arrived in Abbot Creek with the stealth of a mountain cat, the carpet of snow dulling his hoofs to a whisper. He hitched his horse to an oak just outside of town, figuring that he'd risk less chance afoot of being seen shadow-jumping, than in riding along Main. Although his horse's hoofs were silent in the snow, there were men in town who had fought in the Civil War and Indian Wars, with ears attuned to picking up whispers. A rider arriving in a town, at dead of night, no matter how silent his passage, would not go unnoticed. And he had no doubt, too, that a lot of folk would recognize his gait in the saddle. A fall from a horse when he was seven, and the subsequent back injury, gave him a readily recognizable saddle-gait.

Before he set out for the marshal's house, Rick unbuckled the engraved silver spurs he wore, a present from his father the year before to mark his twenty-first birthday. He had worn the spurs every day since, considering them to be his lucky pieces. He put the spurs in his saddle-bag, and then made tracks for the Haskin house. He felt uneasy about leaving the spurs behind, but, in the stillness of the night, there was no way he could wear them without his presence being detected.

He saw two men leaving Wes Lane's house. He hurried ahead of them. He did not know their destination, and wondered why they were carrying cans of kerosene. No doubt they were on one of the judge's nefarious assignments. None of his business, he decided.

Rick reached the marshal's house well ahead of Curly Yokam and his partner. He slid his note under the door and quickly sought the shadows, heading back to his horse by a circuitous route, winding back along the ridge behind Abbot Creek to where he had hitched his horse. Relieved that his task had been completed without incident, he strapped on his silver spurs. He was interrupted by the sudden appearance of a hobo from an alley, and was forced to dive into the shadows. He cursed silently as the buckle of a spur punctured his finger. As soon as the hobo was gone, he mounted up and left Abbot Creek as stealthily as he had arrived.

The next morning he would murder Sam Skelton. Being a man of routine, Sam always took the trail to town through Crazy Gap, where he would be lying in wait. With Drago in or around Crazy Gap, blame for Sam's murder would drop right in his lap.

If Rick Skelton had glanced behind as he rode away, he'd have seen the orange sky as Nate Haskin's house erupted in flames.

Giving up on sleep, Jack Drago acted on his promise to make a cup of coffee and read a book. He was paddling silently across the hall to the shoebox-sized room that Haskin grandiosely called the library, when he spotted the sheet of folded notepaper in the hall. He picked it up and, seeing the name on it, his surprise was total. He opened and read what he assumed to be Beth Crofton's note, his heart winging towards heaven. So overcome with joy was Drago, that he almost missed the smell seeping under the front door.

Kerosene!

There were other sounds, too. *Sloshing*. Footsteps. Muffled gab. Drago's hair stood on end. He tore open the door, just as a match flared to light Danny's ugly dial; his twitching eye danced all over the place on seeing Drago.

Drago grabbed the marshal's gun from the holster hanging on the hallstand, and cut loose with a quick-fire shot that did not find its target, but served to put legs under the arsonist. Drago

126

was about to give chase when another match flared. Out of the shadows at the side of the house, Curly Yokam appeared. Drago spun round, six-gun spitting. Yokam staggered backwards, death haunting his face. As he tottered backwards, the lighting match fell from his jerking fingers.

Drago held his breath.

The match spluttered. Its flame dipped. But it only promised to disappoint. With a sudden flash the match reignited. Trails of orange fire raced towards the house, old lighting new. There were just too many trails to stomp out.

Fingers of flame licked the house and quickly raced up the kerosene-soaked walls. Melting paint from higher up fed the fire. In no time at all, the house was burning from foundation to roof.

Nate Haskin, woken by the gunfire, appeared on the landing in his nightshirt.

'Get Alice,' Drago shouted. 'The house is on fire!'

The marshal dashed into the bedroom and came back immediately carrying a bemused Alice Haskin in his arms. Drago sprinted upstairs to take Alice from Nate. They rushed from the inferno, barely making it through the front door before fire curled through the disintegrating walls. Windows exploded. Flames swept through the rooms. The roof sagged.

Another gun flashed. Danny lurched out of the

darkness clutching his chest. He pointed vaguely behind him and tried to speak. A second bullet in the back pitched him forward on to the flames. The air was acrid with the stench of burning flesh.

Windows were lighting up. Sleepy heads craned out. Men came running with buckets of water. But it was a battle lost. Bewildered, Nate and Alice Haskin stood helpless, watching their home crumble.

'Why would anyone...?' Nate mumbled.

Drago reckoned he had the answer to the lawman's question. The marshal had suddenly got backbone. Alice had stirred a hornets' nest. And he was Haskin's guest. Someone had grasped the opportunity to kill two birds with the one stone, only this time there were three. He also figured that it was the same person who had dispatched the arsonist he had put the run on.

Dead, he could not talk.

Wes Lane retreated deeper into the shadows from which he had shot Danny, standing perfectly still, not daring to draw breath as the citizens of Abbot Creek rushed past on their way to the marshal's house. Lurking within feet of being discovered by a passer-by, Lane began to sweat profusely. If he was detected, he had no answers to give. His plan to eliminate all his problems in one fiery send-off had backfired, and all he had done was add problems to problems. Damn Jack Drago and his night-prowling ways.

He needed time to think.

Taking advantage of a lull in the excitement, as folk commiserated with Nate and Alice Haskin, Wes Lane slunk from cover and door-dodged his way back to his own house. Once inside, with only the merest of pauses to wipe the sweat from his brow, the judge hurried upstairs to his bedroom, where he quickly donned night-attire and ruffled his hair. Then he went to the window and opened it. He poked his head out, rubbing sleepy eyes.

'What's all the excitement about, Andy?' he enquired of a burly man running past.

'Ain't ya got eyes, Judge? The marshal's house has burned down. Shootin', too.'

'Good grief,' Lane said. 'I'd better get along there. See what I can do for those fine people.'

The judge closed the bedroom window, and took deep, relieving breaths. When his skittering nerves settled down, he complimented himself for his fast thinking. He had established that he was in bed. One of the town's most senior and reputable citizens would say so.

Arriving at the scene of the inferno, which by now had almost spent itself, leaving in its wake a charred mess, Wes Lane offered his sympathy to Nate and Alice Haskin.

'Guess you left a lamp still lit, Nate,' he said. 'Happens.'

'The house was in darkness when I came downstairs.'

Lane swung around to face Jack Drago, coming out of the dark.

'This was no accident. The house was torched.' Drago dropped the kerosene can which Danny had left behind at Lane's feet. 'Got any ideas on who might want to do such a thing, Judge?'

Drago went back into the darkness and dragged back Yokam's and Danny's bodies.

'Know these, Lane?'

Wes Lane's brain was spinning.

'Yes. But then the whole town knows them, too.' His gaze flashed across the crowd. 'I'm not denying that they ran errands for me from time to time.' Indignant, as if the thought had just come to him out of the blue, he challenged Drago, 'Are you saying that...?' His hand waved vaguely in the direction of the smouldering house. His indignation leaped. 'How dare you, sir!'

Drago, having acted his way out of many a tight spot in his years of hoboing, saw through Lane's charade.

'I guess that's exactly what I am saying, Lane,' Jack Drago charged stonily. 'I figure you saw a chance to rid yourself of a clutch of thorns in one go.' His tone frosted to zero. 'And you took it.'

130

'Marshal...?' the judge appealed to Haskin.

Lane gambled on the marshal needing clear-cut evidence of any wrongdoing. He'd gambled wisely.

'There's no evidence to back your charge, Jack,' Haskin said.

Wes Lane shot Drago a snide, scoffing look. He turned to the crowd. 'Just as well we have an honest marshal, I say.'

Lane reckoned that his neck was out of a noose, but only temporarily. Later, he'd throw open the saloon. In his experience there was nothing as effective as free whiskey to put a man back on his pedestal. He'd have to rethink his strategy though. Taking direct action to kill Drago and the Haskins was now out of the question. And another accident would be a touch hairy for folk to swallow. He was confident that a way would present itself. Of course, he could always hope for Sam or Rick Skelton to solve the problem for him.

Or, maybe, Spicer McCall?

His eagerness to ingratiate himself with Sam Skelton had made him careless. And a man in his precarious position could not afford to be.

'Nate, Alice,' Lane said, 'you good folk will be my guests until your home is rebuilt.'

'Live under the same roof with you, Wes Lane,' Alice piped up. 'Never!'

Nate Haskin's response to the judge's offer was more measured. 'We can't live under a bush, Alice.'

Alice Haskin's eyes swept the crowd, seeking out an alternative invitation. There was none forthcoming. Everyone knew that having Nate and Alice Haskin as their guests would bring trouble calling. They had allied themselves to Jack Drago. And, therefore, by natural progression, anyone giving them succour would earn Sam Skelton's wrath. No one wanted that kind of grief.

Alice was about to stiffen her opposition to Lane's hospitality, when Jack Drago craftily murmured, 'Once in the castle, Alice, you might discover its secrets.'

Alice, quick as a fox for sensing chicken, changed her stance.

'You know, Judge. I guess I've been a touch hasty and waspish in rejecting your offer of lodgings. Beggars can't be choosers, and that's a fact.'

Alice Haskin's sudden change of mind rocked Wes Lane back on his heels. His invitation to the marshal and his wife hadn't had a smidgen of honesty in it. Now, due to his rash offer, he'd have a lawman under his roof. And worse still, Alice Haskin under his feet!

Nate Haskin murmured in an aside to Jack Drago.

'You know, Drago, you're one foxy gent. You know there ain't a chance in hell of Lane slipping up. But I thank you for getting Alice to see sense.' Concerned, he asked: 'Where will you go?'

'I guess the livery, if the keeper will have me.'

By now Alice had stepped forward jauntily to sling her arm through Wes Lane's, much to everyone's astonishment. Most reckoned, knowing of Alice Haskin's disdain for the judge, that they were witnessing a genuine miracle.

'You being Abbot Creek's most important citizen, we'd best get you inside out of this terrible cold, your honour,' Alice chirped.

'I'll be damned ten times over!' exclaimed the town blacksmith.

'Heck, Gentry,' another man chuckled. 'You've already been damned twelve times or more for dallying with that saloon dove, Babette.'

Al Gentry, being a free man, could take the joshing and even bask in its glory.

The town settled to sleep again. Jack Drago made his way to the livery. Eli Reilly, the livery owner, blocked his path at the gate.

'I wouldn't turn a mangey dog 'way on a night like this, Drago,' he growled. 'But this is a one-night stay, ya understand? Don't want no trouble with Sam or Rick Skelton.'

Drago said: 'I understand, Mr Reilly. I've already decided to ride on tomorrow anyway. I appreciate your kindness, sir.'

'Ride on?' Reilly questioned.

'Yes, sir.'

The livery-owner shook his grizzled head. 'Hell,

133

that sure disappoints me, Drago. I figured you might just be the man to cut Sam Skelton down to size.'

Passing inside the livery, Drago said: 'I've no right to selfishly pursue my claim, if it means trouble for you good folk.'

Eli Reilly snorted. 'Trouble, huh?'

'I reckon so.'

'Mebbe that's what this town needs to shake it 'wake.' He stalked off to a room at the rear of the livery. 'You could've handed this town back its self-respect, Drago. And there you go, runnin' with your tail 'tween your legs.'

He paused before slamming the room door shut.

'It ain't fair, you know.'

'What isn't fair?' Drago asked.

'Stoking Nate Haskin's pride, and then comin' out from under him when he needs you most. That's what ain't fair.' He let out a long, weary sigh. 'I guess if Nate's got any sense he'll go back to bein' deaf, dumb … and blind.'

The door of the room slammed hard enough to shake the rafters. Drago stalked angrily after Reilly and pushed open the door.

'You're scared to have me hanging around for a second night in your damn livery, mister. So you've got no right to climb a pulpit and preach to me!'

Eli Reilly flopped on to the edge of his bunk.

'You know, Drago, you won't understand what I'm about to say until you reach my age. I'm seventy-four. The clock's tickin', and I'm gettin' 'fraid of dyin'.' He snorted. 'Not that I'll be leavin' much behind, other than this flea-pit.'

He became reflective.

'But as your days count down, you begin to treasure them. And you want to hold on to every last one. A young fella like you wouldn't grasp that, 'cause you think you've got lots of time left. And maybe you have, too. But, at seventy-four, you damn well know you ain't.

'Now, some might say that it shouldn't matter none, if you've lived most of your days anyway. But, I tell ya honestly, it does. More and more ev'ry day.' Despondently he said: 'Now git. I need my sleep.'

Drago closed the door. He climbed to the loft where he prepared a bed of straw. Sleep as before, proved elusive. Now he had even more to think about than he'd had in the Haskins' soft feather-bed. Determinedly, he shunted all his thoughts aside, and gave his mind over to Beth Crofton.

THIRTEEN

'Anyone see Rick?' Sam Skelton enquired of several hands as he passed on his way to the stables. All his enquiries brought a negative response. He worried that his bust-up with Rick the night before had made him do something foolish – hothead that he was. On finding Rick's horse missing, his concern notched up.

He had always told Rick that one day there would be Bent Bough cattle on every inch of Tomb Valley range, and had backed that claim with a hard-fist, fast-gun, no-nonsense approach. But, of late, he had got to thinking the way a man does when the years are piling up, about the injustices he had handed out to mainly decent men who wanted nothing more than their fair share. He had begun thinking that, maybe, if he had used his head and his cash instead of his gun and fists to extend the boundaries of the Bent Bough, Beth would not be tied to that drunk Ben Crofton, but

136

be the wife of a man like Jack Drago. Maybe, too, if he had acted differently, Rick would be nearer the man he'd want a son of his to be. Now he was determined to change, and Rick would have to live with that fact.

Sam Skelton mounted up and rode off into the teeth of the ice-laden wind. His desire for change having taken on the zeal of a crusade, it even extended to the route he took to Abbot Creek, changing the habit of a lifetime by not riding through Crazy Gap. However, a short way into the journey nostalgia overtook Sam and he changed trails again. Crazy Gap, in the early days of promise for him and Ellie, had been their favourite dreaming place. They'd sit on the grassy knoll at the top of the gap and look across the valley, seeing cows on Bent Bough range for as far as the eye could see.

'Sneakin' out, huh?'

Jack Drago spun around. Eli Reilly's face was sour with scathing contempt for what he saw as Drago's slinking off. 'Got an errand to do,' Drago said tersely.

'Errand, huh?' Reilly intoned cynically.

'That's what I said,' Drago replied tetchily.

The livery-owner snorted. 'Best you go before Sam Skelton runs you out, I guess.' He cackled.

'Be sure not to trip over that tail 'tween your legs, mister.'

His pride stung, Drago was tempted to reveal the nature of his business. But, bound to secrecy, he had no choice but to let Eli Reilly's poor opinion of him stand.

As he rode away to keep his appointment with Beth Crofton, Jack Drago continued with the speculation of the sleepless night he'd endured, as to why Beth wanted to see him. He'd had fanciful dreams about her being unable to live without him. But in the cold stillness of the morning, his passionate thoughts of the night gone by gave way to less romantic expectations. He concluded that whatever Beth's reason for wanting to meet him, seeing her would be a pleasure-filled start to his day.

Rick Skelton nervously checked his watch. Sam was late. He had not returned to the ranch house, choosing instead to bunk down in a line-shack in the hills, where his sleep was disturbed by the imponderables in his scheme which had surfaced.

What if Jack Drago didn't get the note on time? What if he chose to ignore it? Rick dismissed this notion. He had seen the spark between Beth and Jack Drago. It was as bright as a diamond for anyone to see.

Another possibility had risen up like a grim

spectre to haunt Rick Skelton's night. Could Sam have Jack Drago in mind as a replacement for that dirty old drunk his shiny-clean daughter had got herself hitched to? Was that why he had suddenly gone soft on Drago?

And what if Sam didn't show? What if he had had second thoughts about his grand ideas of equality for all men in Tomb Valley? He was pretty maudlin the night before. Maybe Sam's sudden burst of righteousness had petered out? In that case things would go back to normal. But Rick did not want that to happen. Who knew when Sam would get another loco idea into his head? The Bent Bough, he saw as rightly his, even though he was a wrong side of the blankets son. And he'd be damned if he was going to let Beth Crofton get her hands on it now.

Rick Skelton had fifteen worry-filled minutes before Sam Skelton put in an appearance in the snowy landscape, heading straight for Crazy Gap. His next worry was the arrival of Jack Drago, who was not yet in sight.

Rick massaged his hands to get the circulation going, until they were warm enough to handle the Winchester on a boulder alongside him. When, a couple of minutes after spotting Sam, he caught sight of Jack Drago emerging from a stretch of pine his heart leaped. A natural dip in the trails leading into Crazy Gap would hide Sam and

Drago from each other until they met up in the gap.

Smiling evilly, Rick Skelton hunkered down in the rocks, Winchester at the ready.

'I guess this is the parting of the ways, Daddy,' he murmured.

FOURTEEN

Beth Crofton, her mind rambling and her body fevered, had given up on sleep. At first light she had brewed coffee. She had added a generous helping of whiskey to the coffee and had filled her canteen with the fortified brew, before setting out on the trail to Abbot Creek to plead with Jack Drago to abandon his plans for settling in Tomb Valley. Not that she wanted in any way to see the back of him, far from it. But even if she could control her desire for him, which she wasn't very confident of being able to do, Sam, and particularly Rick Skelton, would remove that temptation from her. So she had decided that the best service she could render Jack Drago was to persuade him to leave right away. In the tiniest corner of her mind, Beth dreamed about Drago asking her to go with him. Though, as yet, she had successfully stifled the notion by repeatedly reminding herself that she was Mrs Ben Crofton for better or for

141

worse until death stepped in, Beth wasn't at all sure of what her reaction would be should Jack Drago make such a proposition.

Beth arrived in Abbot Creek only seconds after Jack Drago had disappeared round the twist in the trail out of town a little way beyond the livery. The time it had taken to run Nate Haskin to ground at Wes Lane's house to find out that Drago had bunked down in Reilly's livery, had put a goodly distance between her and Drago.

'Rode out,' Eli Reilly told Beth. Beth's heart sunk. Reilly scoffed. 'Said he had an errand to do.'

'Errand?' Beth questioned.

'That's what Drago said, ma'am,' the crotchety livery-owner confirmed. 'But I figure he's high-tailed it.'

'What kind of errand?' Beth persisted, finding Reilly's opinion of Jack Drago hard to take.

Eli Reilly shrugged. 'Didn't say.'

'Did he say where this errand was taking him?' Beth asked, fear beginning to stalk her.

'Nope. But ...'

'Yes,' Beth encouraged the thoughtful livery-owner.

'Well, I kinda guess, seein' the trouble brewin' 'tween him and your pa ... Well, ... I was thinkin' ... Maybe Drago would wanna settle accounts with your pa, Beth?'

Beth, her fear now full-blown, swung her horse

142

around and thundered out of town in Drago's wake. She needed to get to the Bent Bough, fast. She picked the trail leading through Crazy Gap.

Jack Drago carefully negotiated the rising trail up to Crazy Gap made treacherous by frozen snow. His full concentration being on the trail, he did not see Sam Skelton until their horses were almost nose to nose. Both men drew rein, each man trying to judge the other's mood. Drago spoke first.

'Howdy, Skelton.'

The Bent Bough boss asked: 'What're you doing out here, Drago?' His tone was sharp.

For a second Drago's hackles rose. 'Riding on,' he lied, seeing no point in telling Skelton about his assignation with his daughter.

The rancher's surprise was total.

'Riding on? Never figured you for a quitter, Drago.'

'There'll be other valleys – more range.'

'Seems to me that you had your heart set on settling here?'

'A man can change his mind.'

Sam Skelton grinned. 'Or have it changed for him.' Drago stiffened in the saddle, his hackles inching up again. 'Settle down. Fact is, I was on my way to town to talk to you.'

'Talk?' Drago snapped. 'What about?'

'About the valley. About sharing it.' Jack Drago's jaw dropped. Skelton snorted. 'Yeah. You heard right, Drago.'

Sam Skelton drew his horse companionably alongside Drago's.

'Folk will say that I'm getting old and losing my grip. But the fact is that for some time now, I've grown tired of gunplay and fisticuffs.' His eyes wandered across the expanse of Tomb Valley. 'I still want to own every blade of grass in this valley. But I reckon the time has come to buy out other men's claims, if they want to sell. Or else to share the range with them as neighbours.'

'That'll shackle the boundaries of the Bent Bough,' Drago observed.

'It will, and I'll be dependent on my neighbours' grass for a spell until the Bent Bough herd can be fed within its own boundaries. But,' he said doggedly, 'it's time to make a darn start to ending the feuding which has stalked this range for far too long.'

He settled a steady and friendly gaze on Jack Drago. 'Go and stake your claim, Drago.' The rancher held out his hand to shake. 'Welcome to the valley ... neighbour.'

Jack Drago took Sam Skelton's hand and shook it warmly. But his joy was short-lived. There was another problem in the valley that, as things stood, could not be resolved.

'Thank you for your neighbourliness, Skelton,' Drago said. 'But I'll be moving on anyway.'

Sam Skelton studied Drago for a long time before he spoke. 'Beth, ain't it?' he asked bluntly.

Jack Drago's first instinct was to deny his feelings for Beth Crofton. But with the rancher looking deep into his soul, he figured that it would be a waste of breath and time to do so.

'I saw the spark between you two,' Sam stated. 'So bright that it would pierce a blind man's eyes.'

'Then you'll understand why I must ride on, sir,' Drago said.

Sam Skelton said: 'Yes. I do. Land is one thing to grab, but a man's wife ... Well, that's something else.'

Drago's spirits plummeted to their lowest. A small part of him had hoped that Sam would give his blessing to Beth and him as a couple. But the code of not taking another man's wife, no matter what the circumstances, was too ingrained in Westerners for that hope to have had a chance. Times, Drago had heard, were changing in other places. But the West, being the raw land it still was, would take time to catch up with newfangled liberties.

Jack Drago got one speck of consolation from Sam Skelton's next statement.

'If it was possible that you and Beth could be mates, I'd give the union my blessing, Drago.'

145

The two men, unaware of having Rick Skelton as an eavesdropper, only became aware of his presence when his rifle cracked and spun Sam Skelton out of his saddle. Drago, surprise working against him, had his gun clearing leather when Rick Skelton's Winchester spat again. Drago felt the burn of lead on his forehead, and a red cloud spread across his eyes. His head buzzed with the thunder of Rick Skelton's bullet as he toppled from the saddle nose-diving into the rocks. Blackness rushed in on him.

Seconds later, Rick Skelton crept from his bushwhacker's hidey-hole higher up in the gap, to examine his handiwork. He had shot his father in the back, but it gave him no qualms of conscience. The only thought occupying his mind right now was to cover his crime.

He took Sam Skelton's gun from its holster and fired off a couple of shots. Then he did the same with Drago's, to convey the impression that there had been a gunfight between the two men.

On hearing gunfire in the silent landscape, Beth Crofton drew rein, her fear raw and pulsating. The shooting had, she reckoned, come from Crazy Gap. Was she too late? Had Jack Drago clashed with Bent Bough riders? Or her father? Beth's heart thumped heavily in her chest. If that were

146

the case, then she could only be facing grief if Jack
Drago was dead. And surprisingly, she found that
she would grieve too, should it be her father's
body she found. Her grief would be different, but
it would be a sorrow as keenly felt. Overcoming
her shock, Beth spurred her horse in a mad gallop
to Crazy Gap.

Rick Skelton, surprised by Beth's appearance,
had to scramble through the rocks and barely
cleared the gap before she thundered into it. In
the morning stillness, her wail of agony reached
far across the valley. Rick slipped quietly away. He
rode a rambling route back to the Bent Bough. On
his arrival, he craftily enquired as to Sam
Skelton's whereabouts.

'Gone to town to square things with Drago,' Ned
Rawlson told Rick.

A credible actor, Rick's astonishment came
across as genuine. 'Square things with Drago?' he
chuckled. 'Why, Ned, you must have got the wrong
end of the stick.' He promoted his chuckle to
laughter. 'Pa, squaring things with Dra…? If that
ain't the craziest thing I ever heard.'

Still laughing, Rick let his horse amble on to
the stables, where, on entering, he was careful to
be still laughing.

Lanky Doyle, the old-timer sweeping out the
stables, asked: 'What's ticklin' your ribs, Rick?'

Rick swung down from his horse, shaking his

head. 'The craziest thing ...' He confided Ned Rawlson's message to Doyle.

The old-timer laughed toothlessly. 'Sam Skelton toleratin' an interloper? Never heard such rubbish.'

'That's what I figure too, Lanky.' Then, seeing an opportunity to sow a seed, he said with the right measure of concern: 'Sure hope Pa will be safe.'

Rick handed the reins to the old man. He left Lanky Doyle to ponder on the fear he'd just raised. He strolled across the yard to the ranch house, careful to maintain his mood of concern, a mood that vanished the second he got inside the house. He wandered along the hall, pausing to look into the rooms, rooms which were now his alone, until he arrived at the den, which he entered. He poured himself a stiff drink, and flopped into Sam Skelton's cowhide chair. He took a long, easy slug of the Kentucky rye, washing it about his mouth to savour its warm glow and smooth quality, before letting the liquid slide down his throat.

He looked across the room at a painting of Sam and Ellie Skelton holding the reins of a coal-black stallion, gazing out across the range at a content-edly munching herd. Rick's anger flared. He sprang out of his chair and tore the painting off the den wall. He hurled the portrait across the room, and when it fell to the floor he danced maniacally on it.

'I'm boss of the Bent Bough now,' he ranted. 'And I'll decide what hangs on the walls!'

He again threw himself into Sam Skelton's chair. All he had to do now was sit tight and wait for Beth to come running with the bad news of her father's murder. Then he'd ride out, as any grieving son would, to hang his pa's murderer. He took pride in the slickness of his plan. At last the Bent Bough and Tomb Valley were his.

So, why was he suddenly feeling so uneasy?

Nerves were natural, Rick Skelton told himself. The jitters would soon pass. *All you've got to do is sit pretty and be outraged.* He replenished his glass and hoisted his boots on to the desk, disdainfully rolling a spur along its highly polished surface, leaving behind an ugly scar. He slugged down a generous gulp of rye, and almost choked. He knew in a flash the source of his unease. On reflection it had niggled at him as he had crossed the yard from the stables.

Blood drained from Rick Skelton's face, leaving behind a dirty grey pallor.

Jack Drago heard what he thought to be a rush of water in his ears as he came to. There was a drum beating inside his head, from the raw, throbbing graze running almost the full length of his forehead. His recollection of what had happened rushed back. His eyes shot open.

He was looking into Beth Crofton's gun barrel.

FIFTEEN

'Get up slowly,' Beth ordered Jack Drago, her tone harshly uncompromising. 'Blink and I'll finish what my father started.'

Drago saw Sam Skelton's prone figure.

'I didn't shoot your father, Beth.'

'Get on your horse.'

Angered by Beth's doubting him, but also understanding how it looked, he said: 'Sam and I were bushwhacked.'

'Bushwhacked?'

'Yes.'

'By whom?'

'Obviously by someone who wanted us both out of the way, Beth. The man who got me out here. And who knew your father would also be here.'

Unconvinced, Beth scoffed. 'That's the tallest yarn I've heard for a long time, Mr Drago.'

Jack Drago was putting together the pieces of a very intricate plot. Damn. If only he hadn't thrown away the note which was supposed to have come from Beth but which he was now certain was the work of the bushwhacker.

'You didn't write a note asking me to meet you here, did you Beth?'

'Note? What note?'

'The note that got me out here, to make this possible.'

'On your horse, Drago,' she ordered. 'Tell your cock-and-bull yarn to Marshal Haskin.' She snorted. 'I reckon he'll think it's got as much moss as I do.'

'It's the truth, Beth,' Jack Drago said quietly. 'Give me a chance, and I'll prove it.'

'Give you the chance to hit a fast trail, you mean,' Beth said scornfully. 'Now, get on your horse or I'll shoot you where you stand!'

As Beth Crofton mounted her horse, holding a gun on Jack Drago, her emotions were cartwheeling. She had lost her father, and was now about to lose the man who had meant so much to her.

Jack Drago too had his regrets. Life sure had taken the sourest twist of all, in a long trail of sour twists.

As they rode away, Drago's eye caught a glint of something bright in the rocks, where the weak sun had just poked through. He drew rein.

'Just a minute, Beth.'

Rifle ready, Beth covered every inch of Drago's

journey to where his eye had caught the glint. He stooped and picked up a silver spur.

Back at the Bent Bough, Rick Skelton's eyes were wide with horror. He cursed. He was missing a spur. He recalled his frantic scramble through the rocks in Crazy Gap when Beth put in her unexpected appearance. He must have lost it then. It was the single spur's jangling music that had registered with him crossing the yard; he had grown used to a double jangle.

Rick's mind raced back further to the night before when he had been surprised by the hobo in Abbot Creek, and his hurried buckling of the spurs. The spur could have fallen off anywhere. But he was betting that he had lost it back in Crazy Gap. Maybe it would never be found? But what if it was? He'd have to go back and search every inch of Crazy Gap, if he wanted to sleep nights.

Beth Crofton held the silver spur in her hand, her eyes riveted to the engraved initials: RS.

Drago said: 'That spur hasn't been here for long, Beth. It's dry. No signs of weathering either.' He straightened up from his examination of a boulder near where he'd found the spur. 'Fresh scratch-marks on this boulder, too. All the signs point to Rick having murdered Sam.'

153

Beth staggered. Drago grabbed hold of her and cradled her to him.

'Why would Rick murder Sam, Jack?' Beth whimpered.

'Because your father was set on new ways, Beth.'

'New ways?'

Drago relayed to Beth what had taken place between him and Sam Skelton.

'Father was willing to let you settle in Tomb Valley?' Beth asked in disbelief.

'Yes. He was,' Drago confirmed.

Beth's eyes flooded. 'That's good to know, Jack.'

Unable to resist the urge that stole the strength from her legs, Beth was in Jack Drago's arms and kissing him. Going against every urge and emotion in him, he pushed her back to arm's length.

'Beth,' he said solemnly, 'it isn't fair to give a man a hankering which he can never satisfy.'

'You could,' she said, desperately.

Drago said: 'I'm as tempted as Adam ever was. But, like it not, you're another man's wife, Beth. Besides, I won't be around.'

'Not around,' she asked, puzzled. 'But you said that Sam—'

'So he did. But how am I supposed to stay in the valley and see you most days, Beth? Even a part of this fine range isn't enough of a prize to

154

lose my sanity for.'

'But, Jack—'

He put a finger to her pleading lips. 'We'd both go loco, Beth.' He shook his head with dogged finality. 'No good could come of me hanging around.'

Beth Crofton's shoulders slumped in resignation. She knew the truth of what Jack Drago said. Being in the same valley would be like mixing oil with flame. Drago held Beth gently.

'I've been waiting all my life for a chance, Beth,' he said. 'I wasn't even sure of what that chance might be. And now that I've found it ...' He turned and strode to his horse. 'I'll head back to town. Clear my name with Nate Haskin.'

He vaulted into the saddle. He looked at Sam Skelton's body draped across his saddle.

'I know it doesn't seem like it now, Beth,' he said. 'But I reckon some good will come of all of this.'

He turned to ride away, when, through a gap in the rocks, he saw a rider coming fast towards Crazy Gap. Though he was not yet near enough to recognize, Jack Drago had no doubt about the rider's identity. He dismounted and took Beth and her horse into the rocks out of sight. Then he returned to lay Sam Skelton's body where he'd fallen. Both his own and Skelton's horses he left where they had been when Rick Skelton was last in the gap. Drago then went to lie where Beth had found him. The stage was set.

On his arrival, Rick Skelton jumped from his horse and began a frantic search for his lost spur. Drago stood up, knocking the wind from Rick's sails. He held out the initialled silver spur.

'This what you're looking for, Rick?'

Skelton's gimlet eyes took in the entire gap in a blink. Deciding that Drago was alone, his hand dived for his gun. He held the Colt .45 on Drago.

'Seems like I didn't do a good enough job the last time,' he snarled. 'Mighty generous of you to hand me another chance, Drago. Which I won't waste.'

'Drop the gun, Rick.'

Beth's snapped order had Rick Skelton reeling. She came from the rocks, holding Rick under the threat of her Winchester. His plans to grab the Bent Bough down the drain, Rick lost all reason. His gun barked. Drago grabbed Beth about the waist and they went down heavily. Skelton's second bullet buzzed off a rock inches from Drago's face. Drago grabbed a rock and threw it at Skelton. It missed, but the seconds it took Skelton to duck and come back shooting was all that Jack Drago needed. His six-gun flashed in his hand, and Rick Skelton teetered backwards, fatally wounded, still intent on mayhem. Drago's second bullet went zinging Rick Skelton's way with deadly effect, shattering his chest bone and exploding his heart.

Shocked by the horror before her eyes, Beth Crofton clung to Jack Drago.

EPILOGUE

By early spring the Haskin house was rebuilt.
Jack Drago worked hard at making it happen, as
did most of the townsmen. There was a new feeling to life in Abbot Creek. Judge Wes Lane, his
ticket to Washington cancelled, had tried to flee
town, but Nate Haskin had nailed him. Spicer
McCall had ridden like the wind when Rick
Skelton was toppled. Nate and Alice, along with
many others, had asked Jack Drago to stay. But
by now most folk knew why he could not.

With the spring days warming, Jack Drago
swung into the saddle, said his goodbyes and rode
away. The thunder of hoofs arriving in town had
him drawing rein. He turned in the saddle to see
Beth Crofton riding like the wind along Main. She
drew rein alongside Drago.

'Jack Drago,' she said. 'You might be willing to
let your chance slip by. But I'm sure as hell not.
I'm leaving with you.'

'Leaving with me?' he yelped.

'That's what I said.'

'But the ranch, Beth? And Ben?'

'The Bent Bough has a good foreman in Ned Rawlson, until the day we can return to the valley. And I never loved Ben Crofton.'

Drago tempered his excitement.

'No, Beth,' he said resolutely. 'The Bent Bough and Ben both need you.'

It was rumoured around town that Ben Crofton's drinking was fast catching up with him.

'I'll be back this way,' Drago promised Beth. Jack Drago sat ramrod straight in the saddle as he rode out of Abbot Creek. The way a man can, when he leaves with pride.

It was a year later. Jack Drago had just ridden into a small, no-consequence Arizona town, just as the bank was being robbed. There was a man, dressed in preacher's garb, shooting back into the bank, shouting that the bank was being robbed.

Drago chuckled. The reverend swung around.

'Old ways die hard, Reverend,' Drago said.

Jack Drago's Colt .45 spat. This time, Spicer McCall did not make it across the border.